Adoring
Stacey

Elsa Winckler

Adoring Stacey
Copyright © 2023 Elsa Winckler
All rights reserved.

ISBN: (ebook) 978-1-958136-25-6
(print) 978-1-958136-26-3

Inkspell Publishing
207 Moonglow Circle #101
Murrells Inlet, SC 29576

Edited By Rie Langdon
Cover Art By Fantasia Frog

DEDICATION

To our son Johan for all his love and support

ELSA WINCKLER

CHAPTER 1

"I simply have to talk to Stacey, right now!" Eleanor Johnson's voice carried right to the back of the shop where Stacey Lawrence happened to be working in her office. "I've been here twice already this morning."

Swallowing a soft groan, Stacey got up and walked to the front of her printing-slash-design-slash-handling-computer-related-problems shop.

"Oh, Stacey, there you are!" Eleanor beamed and rushed closer, her arms outstretched, ready for a hug. "I've just been telling Billie here it's urgent that I talk to you. It seems I keep missing you today."

Guiltily, Stacey returned the older woman's hug. It wasn't that she didn't like Eleanor Johnson. In fact, she loved talking to the flamboyant, funny, and endearing local artist, but besides the fact that she was crazy busy on this freezing last Friday of October, she was also extremely wary of Eleanor's self-proclaimed matchmaking skills.

As a very happy single woman, her biggest frustration since moving to Alisson, Montana two years before was that everyone in this town, especially Eleanor, seemed bent on finding her the one thing she seriously didn't want: a husband.

When she'd arrived here, two of the first people she'd met were the two Wilson sisters, Charlie and Lindsay, both local businesswomen. It had been such a surprise to discover that they, like Stacey, were also originally from South Africa.

Over the last two years, Charlie had married Eleanor's son Logan and Lindsay had married Blake Davidson, an ex-FBI agent who was now one of the owners of the local dojo in town.

Eleanor's daughter Brooke, also a renowned artist, had married Charlie and Lindsay's brother Gavin, and he'd subsequently moved to Alisson during the past year. Although Eleanor had never admitted she'd played any active role in these love matches, the town gossip mill was full of stories of how she'd wrangled things to get the couples together.

Eleanor had been shamelessly inquisitive about Stacey's history ever since her arrival in town, but so far, she'd managed to evade the older woman's questions by offering simple, vague answers with a smile. Even though Stacey preferred not to think of the past—it wasn't as if she had anything to hide—but she'd quickly picked up on Eleanor's not-so-subtle-attempts to try and find her a husband.

So, the less Stacey talked about her herself, the quicker Eleanor would find a new subject to try her matchmaking skills on, she'd reasoned. However, since Brooke and Gavin had tied the knot in June earlier that year, it was clear Eleanor had turned the focus of her skills on Stacey with renewed gusto, something that made Stacey even more wary.

"I need your help, dear," Eleanor was saying.

Stacey smiled tentatively. "As long as it's not about dating anyone, I'm happy to help."

Eleanor sighed dramatically. "You are one of the most beautiful women I've ever seen. With all that glorious red hair and your beautiful sapphire blue eyes, you have all the single men—and, I'm afraid, even some not-so-single men—in this town just about salivating after you—"

Rolling her eyes, Stacey groaned out loud to stop her. "Seriously, Eleanor, I've—"

"Don't worry," Eleanor interrupted, seemingly resigned. "I know. I've received the message: you're happily single. I've given up hope to get you married, so you can relax. My matchmaking skills are obviously not working on you. I'm here to ask if you can make posters for the Bachelor Auction."

Stacey laughed in surprise. "Bachelor Auction? Are you serious? I didn't know that was actually a thing."

Eleanor patted her arm. "It's a fun way to fundraise, my dear. The town hasn't done it in ages, but when the mayor asked what we could do to raise money for some of the local kids who want to go to college and can't afford it, someone suggested a Bachelor Auction. Everyone was keen on the idea. We're hoping to rope in all the bachelors in town and on the neighboring ranches. We don't have much time; it must be done before all the Christmas festivities start, so it's to be held in three weeks in the town hall and we need to advertise the event, hence the need for posters. And of course, we'll need pictures of all of our bachelors taking part. Would you mind doing that for us? You take such lovely pictures…"

"Do you think that's necessary?" Brooke asked, finally speaking up. "You could do an eye-catching poster with maybe silhouettes, or—"

"Oh, no, my dear," Eleanor smiled. "We want to flaunt our bachelors. Alisson boasts so many attractive, single men and I think it's time to let them shine, don't you?"

"Whatever you say," Brooke replied. "Although texting everyone an invite would probably be quicker and cheaper."

Eleanor winked at Billie. "See? This is why I came to see you. Stacey will know what to do: I've told everyone on the committee. That's a brilliant idea! Thank you, my dear. I do think, though, that there should also be a few posters we can put up around town. And could you perhaps take pictures of our bachelors tomorrow? I'll of course arrange with the bachelors to come to your shop? I know you're not open every Saturday, but we don't have much time. We could put up posters at Lindsay's shop, for instance, the coffee shop, the pharmacy and..." She snapped her fingers. "I know—what about the dojo? Now that Jason is co-owner with Blake, you can also ask him if you can't get hold of Blake. Lately, just about everyone I know goes for self-defense classes, or whatever other martial arts they fancy. It just makes sense to have a poster in their window. What do you think?"

Ignoring the slight tug at her heart at the mention of Jason Coleman's name, Stacey swallowed a groan. And there it was: Eleanor never talked to her without mentioning Jason's name at least once. You had to be both deaf and blind not to see what the older woman was up to.

Stacey was all business, though; she was not going to react to Jason's name. "Okay, yes. We can do the posters for you and text the ad to everyone on our mailing list. Billie here won't mind putting up the posters, you just let her know where. Let's sit down over here at the table and you can tell me what you had in mind."

An hour later, when Eleanor left, she was all smiles. Billie chuckled. "You do know that she's going to get you to bid on one of the bachelors, don't you?"

"Over my dead body," Stacey muttered as she stomped to the back where her studio was.

"Not even on Jason Coleman?" Billie's amused voice followed her all the way.

Especially not on Jason Coleman. Irritated, Stacey opened her laptop. It didn't matter that the tall, broad-shouldered ex-FBI agent was drop-dead gorgeous, she was not looking for a boyfriend or a husband.

Not even a lover? The pesky little voice inside, always irritating her, wanted to know.

The image of Jason's broad shoulders flashed in front of her, heating her blood. Groaning, she tried to fan herself with the paper she held in her hand. She had work to do. She was not going to entertain thoughts of Jason Coleman, no matter how ridiculously hot he was.

Oh, my goodness, there you go again. It was time to get some fresh air. Grabbing her coat, she made for the front door. Billie was on her phone, as she very often was, so Stacey motioned to her she was going to get a coffee.

The October air was freezing cold. Huddling in her coat, she glanced up at the snow-tipped mountains as she crossed the street. The bitter cold of the Montana winters had been the one thing she'd struggled with when she'd first arrived. Winters in South Africa were mild compared to the extreme temperatures in Alisson.

Over the past year, though, she had come to appreciate the slowdown of life during the cold months. As an avid reader, she enjoyed being holed up over weekends with a book, a hot chocolate, and a warm fire. There was nobody else she needed to take care of, an absolutely blissful thought.

She'd finally found a place where she could settle, where she lived a simple life, one without complications or friction. That was why it had been important to her to make success of her small business. She wasn't rolling in money, but she determined what she did each day and how much she wanted to do. Never again did she want to be in a position where someone else could dictate what she should do—and shouldn't do.

A car horn blared just as she entered the coffee shop, making her glance behind her. The next moment, she walked directly into a brick wall. A big hand folded around her arm. Even before she looked up, she knew it must be Jason Coleman. There was just something in the air when he was around.

"Uhm… sorry," she muttered, and tried to move around him, but he stayed where he was.

"Good morning, Stacey," he said, his voice sending delicious shivers down her spine.

Seriously, whatever was the matter with her? Granted, Jason was swoon-worthy, but she was a grown woman, not a schoolgirl, for heaven's sake. She didn't *actually* have to swoon now, did she?

"Jason." She nodded and again tried to move past him.

"Oh, Jason!" Eleanor's voice rang out behind her. "There you are—I've been looking for you!" She smiled while catching her breath. "And here is Stacey as well. Perfect timing. Have you told him, my dear?" she asked, looking at Stacey.

"Told me what?" asked Jason.

"About the Bachelor Auction," Eleanor said, her whole body vibrating with excitement. "Stacey is doing our marketing and has agreed to make some posters for the event. We were wondering whether she could put one up on one of the windows at the dojo. And you will, of course, sign up to be one of our bachelors, won't you? All the gorgeous single women in town, like our Stacey here, will be there to bid on their bachelor of choice. We're raising funds to help kids who can't afford to go to college, so you can't say no." While talking, she whipped out a book and pen. "I'm adding your name to the list. Thanks so much, Jason!" And blowing kisses, she rushed down the street.

Stunned, Jason stared after Eleanor's retreating figure. "What just happened?"

"I think you've been conned into taking part in the bachelor auction," Stacey said, her eyes dancing with mirth.

Intrigued, Jason looked down at the gorgeous redhead who, much to his irritation, had been invading his dreams since he'd first laid eyes on her. He didn't think he'd ever seen her smiling, at least not when he was around. "Seems to me I'm not the only one who's been conned."

"Oh, I'm just helping with the marketing, I know what I'm doing."

"Is that right?" he drawled. "I'm pretty sure I've heard her say you'll be one of the...how did she put it? Oh, yes, 'gorgeous single women in town, like our Stacey here, will be there to bid on their bachelor of choice.'"

"Bid on a *date* with a bachelor," she said. "And I'm not bidding. I want to get a coffee. Do you mind...?"

"Wanna bet?"

"Yes, I'll even bet on it. You won't get me near the event—"

"Okay, here's the bet. If Eleanor succeeds and you do bid, I get to take you out on a date."

He narrowed his eyes ever so slightly. "Don't be ridiculous."

"Chicken?"

Rolling her eyes, Stacey groaned. "Seriously. Okay, if I take your bet, will you please move so I can get a coffee?"

"So what do you want if you do succeed in not bidding?"

"I..." Her eyes lit up. "Oh, I know." She chuckled. "If I don't bid, which I won't, you have to sing a song."

"Sing a song?"

Fascinated, he stared at her. Her eyes were actually twinkling.

"Yes. At the end of the auction. I'll make sure I'm on time to hear that. Could you please move?"

He did. With an exasperated sigh, Stacey stomped into the coffee shop. As she walked past him, he caught a whiff of her scent, camellias. And his body reacted.

After nearly a year, he finally had a name for the fragrance always enveloping her. It had taken him the best part of a morning during his last visit to Bozeman, and he had to sniff every damn bottle of perfume at the counter in one of the big stores in town, but eventually he was able to identify the perfume she wore, the smell that had been driving him crazy ever since he'd met her. Camellias.

Grimacing, he slowly walked toward his truck. What the hell was wrong with him? He liked women, he enjoyed them—their softness, their strengths, their curves—but he always kept it light and made sure every woman he spent time with knew from the start he wasn't interested in anything more permanent.

Marriage, kids—those had never been possibilities he'd even considered. His experience of his parents' marriage had left a bitter taste in his mouth. His decision had never bothered him. No woman came close to making him re-think his future.

But then on a perfectly ordinary day, Stacey Lawrence had happened.

He'd first seen her when he'd agreed to temporarily help out at his friend Blake Davidson's dojo. Like Jason, Blake was also ex-FBI, and had moved to the small town of Alisson and opened a dojo, where he taught martial arts and self-defense classes.

When Blake had decided to go on another mission for the FBI, he'd contacted Jason to ask if he'd take over the running of the dojo and the classes in Blake's absence. At the time, Jason had been looking to buy a ranch and had readily agreed, thinking that while he was in Alisson, he'd have time to decide where he wanted to live the rest of his life.

Turned out, Montana was full of surprises. Not only did he end up buying a ranch outside of Alisson, but he'd also met Stacey Lawrence.

She'd been in the very first self-defense class he'd taught. He'd immediately zoomed in on the tall woman standing in the back of the class: red curls tumbling down a slender back, a mouth-watering sexy body with curves in all the right places, toned legs that seemed to go on forever. The unexpected fist of desire in his gut had nearly brought him to his knees.

And that was before he'd looked into her blue eyes, the

color of a Montana sky on a clear day.

With his gaze still on the entrance of the coffee shop, Jason got into his truck.

His arrangement with Blake had begun as a temporary one, but here he was, a year later, and not only had he become part owner of the dojo with Blake, he had a ranch adjacent to the one where the Johnson and Wilson families were now all living. He had settled, he had made this place his home.

Blake and his wife Lindsay shared the ranch with Lindsay's sister, Charlie, her husband Logan, Logan's sister Brooke, and her husband Gavin, who was also Lindsay and Charlie's brother—and of course that was where Eleanor Johnson lived, not just Logan and Charlie's mother but the self-declared matchmaker of Alisson.

He leaned forward to start the truck but just then Stacey exited the coffee shop. Dropping his hand, he leaned back to watch her. With long, no-nonsense strides, long red curls swinging from side to side over her back, she crossed the street.

Why would a gorgeous woman like her have moved oceans to live and work here, in this particular small town?

Of course, he'd heard the gossip. Like Lindsay and her sister Charlie had done, she'd relocated from South Africa. Charlie had inherited her aunt's house and business, and Lindsay had been trying to get away from an abusive boyfriend, so their reasons for emigrating he could understand. Stacey's reasons, though, were still unknown, much to the frustration of the gossip mill in Alisson. She was friendly and helpful, but clammed up whenever people started asking questions about her past.

She also didn't date. At least not in Alisson. It was known that at times she visited Bozeman, but as far as he knew—and for some reason he made it his business to know about all things Stacey Lawrence—she also didn't see anyone while she visited the city.

Of course, the gossip mill had been wondering whether

the lovely Ms. Lawrence didn't prefer women, but he'd bet singing another damn song she didn't. That very first day in the dojo? He hadn't been the only one affected. In that first moment their eyes had met he'd seen the changes in her body even after she'd quickly tried to cover up her breasts with another top.

He hadn't liked the way his whole being had focused on her, how he'd been aware of her every move and how, for a split second he'd imagined her on his ranch, playing with a little red-haired girl and a damn dog yapping at their feet. Freaked-out didn't come close to describe the near-panic attack he'd had. He would know. While he'd been in the field as an FBI agent, he'd been familiar with this feeling.

So he'd tried his best to stay as far away from her as possible. It had worked quite well, because as he'd discovered, she was also doing her best to avoid him at all costs. She'd stopped coming to self-defense classes and whenever he spotted her in town or at some or other function, she'd duck and disappear quickly. It had been too obvious not to notice.

Irritated with himself, he started his truck. Even if he had an excellent foreman he relied on, he had a ranch to tend to.

The truck hiccupped, coughed a few times before it started. Patting the dashboard, he coaxed it. "Come on, Maggie-girl, you can do it." Sighing in relief when the truck started, he stepped on the gas.

He had a brand-new truck on the ranch and it was probably time to just leave this pile of metal to become one with nature, but it had been his grandpa's truck since he could remember and okay, yeah, he had trouble letting it go. Anyway, Maggie-girl was still moving, wasn't she?

Maybe it was a good idea to visit the bar tonight. He hadn't been in town on a Friday night for ages, hadn't been with a woman for...damn, he couldn't even remember for how long. One thing he knew for sure—he wouldn't run into the lovely Ms. Lawrence. She was seldom seen in the local bar. Rumor had it she preferred to stay at home reading.

Cussing, he put his foot on the gas and sped out of town. He was all hot and bothered while she went about her daily routine as if nothing had happened.

Nothing *had* happened. He'd just bet her she would bid on him. And if she didn't, he'd have to sing. The slow smile started deep within his belly.

Well, she was in for a surprise, no matter what the outcome of the auction.

ELSA WINCKLER

CHAPTER 2

The moment Stacey stepped into Suds Stop on Friday night, she regretted agreeing to Lindsay's invitation to join them. The whole freaking town seemed to be in the bar. Before she could turn around and flee as she wanted to, Lindsay saw her and rushed over.

"Stacey!" she called out and hugged her. "I'm so glad to see you. Ever since Laney was born, I haven't been anywhere. It feels like forever since I've last seen you. Come on, we've managed to grab two tables just in time— it's Friday night and everyone is here. Mom is babysitting Charlie and Logan's Elly and our Laney. Connor has announced he's way too old to be babysat at the ripe old age of seven, but he's helping Granny."

There wasn't much else to do but follow Lindsay to the area where the rest of the Johnson and Wilson clan were sitting.

As she neared the table, she heard someone laugh. Her gaze moved toward the sound even before she registered what she was doing. Jason Coleman was leaning against the bar, laughing down at one of the waitresses.

In that instant, he looked up, catching her gaze on him. For a moment, everything around her faded, all she was aware of was those deep blue eyes looking right into her very soul. Blinking, she quickly turned her back on him and greeted the others. Unnerved, she sat down on the first available chair.

Around her, people were talking and laughing but although she was also smiling, she had no idea what was being said. Her whole being was still in the moment Jason's gaze had met hers.

Damn it, what was happening? She'd been trying to ignore him for the past year. The feeling would pass, just like it normally did, she kept telling herself. Jason wasn't the first man to stir something inside of her.

He was, however, the first man she couldn't seem to get out of her mind and her dreams, no matter how hard she tried.

Love made people do stupid things, as she'd noticed while watching the people around her. These crazy feelings could be explained. As she usually did when she didn't understand something, she'd researched it. Turned out this woozy feeling one experienced upon meeting an attractive guy like Jason was just biology. Hormones. It would pass.

Okay, at this point it was clear it was going to take a little longer than usual, but it would pass eventually. The important thing was she had to make sure she didn't do anything stupid while her dopamine and norepinephrine levels were still sky-high.

These chemicals, as her research had shown, made people giddy, energetic, and euphoric, even leading to decreased appetite and insomnia—which meant you could actually be so "in love" that you couldn't eat and couldn't sleep. At least she knew why her appetite was gone and why her dreams were constantly filled with vivid images of a near-naked Jason. Not that she'd seen him naked, of course, but the tight T-shirts he wore in summer gave her a pretty good idea of what was beneath the thin material.

Aaargh, she was still thinking about him! Damn it, she was not *ever* going to be roped into a life of babies and endless washing and cooking and demands on her time, no matter how gorgeous Jason was.

She had a vague memory of a happy childhood while her parents had still been alive. But the subsequent nightmare years after they'd both died when a freak wave took them from her—they'd all been on a holiday at the sea—had just about wiped that memory from her mind. She shook away the memories and tried to concentrate on the scene around her.

The moment her insides finally settled, the chair next to her was pulled out roughly. Even before she turned her head, she knew it was Jason. She got goosebumps—seriously, what twenty-seven-year-old woman still got goosebumps because of a man? A kaleidoscope of butterflies in her tummy went crazy and her mouth dried out.

"Hi, everybody. Seems the whole town is here," he said to no one in particular.

"Hi, Jason," Charlie called out cheerily, her gaze going between Jason and Stacey. "Everyone is talking about the upcoming Bachelor Auction. Mom tells me you've signed up?"

Jason grimaced. "Not quite how I see it. I was signed up. I didn't really have a choice."

"Smart man," Logan joked. "Even if you'd refused, my mother would've pestered you mercilessly."

Jason leaned back in his chair. "Well, it's for a good cause." He chuckled. "And Stacey here has agreed to bid on me—"

"I did no such thing!" Stacey interrupted him hotly. "I've even made a bet with you I won't bid on you, or anyone else!" The moment the words left her mouth, she realized she'd walked into his trap. She'd just told everyone about her conversation with Jason—the very last thing she wanted people to talk about. Every eye around the table was on her.

Inhaling sharply, Lindsay leaned forward. "What was

the bet?"

"It was…it was nothing, really." Stacey tried, but she should've known she'd never get off so easily.

"Oh, come on!" Charlie cajoled. "We're old married women looking for some excitement."

Brooke, about six months pregnant, laughed. "Does my mom know about this bet?"

"No!" Stacey called out. "And please don't tell her, I beg you. I'll never hear the end of it. Ever since I've arrived in Alisson, she's been trying to set me up with every available man around, especially Jason…" With a soft groan, she dropped her head in her hands. "I can't believe I've just said that."

Next to her, Jason's whole body was shaking with laughter.

"It's not funny!" she snapped, glaring at him.

"Oh, it's funny." He laughed. "Okay, I'll tell you what happened. I bet Stacey here Eleanor is going to make sure she bids on a bachelor."

"What was the bet?" Charlie asked.

"If she does bid on me or someone else, I get to take her on a date," Jason said.

Lindsay's eyes widened. "And if she doesn't?"

Jason shifted uncomfortably on his chair. "Well, that's not gonna happen."

"Ha, not so funny when the joke's on you, is it?" Stacey laughed. "If I don't put in a bid, which I won't, he has to sing a song at the end of the auction in front of everyone."

Blake's eyes widened and he laughed. "I gather she doesn't know…?" He winked at Jason.

"Know what?" Lindsay asked.

But Blake's eyes just twinkled.

Exasperated, Stacey looked from Blake to Jason. Something was up but she didn't want to know about it anyway. She'd had enough. Jumping up, she grabbed her purse. "I'm getting a beer. Anyone else?"

Everyone wanted another one. To her chagrin, Jason

joined her as she walked toward the bar.

"You didn't have to tell everyone about the bet, seriously," she said crossly. "And I don't need your help. I'll get a tray. I've done my share of waitressing."

But he continued grinning. "See? We're finally getting to know one another. I didn't know you'd been a waitress before you moved to Alisson."

She stopped in the middle of the bar and faced him. "I don't know what your game is, but—"

But before she could finish her sentence, his hand reached out and warm fingers touched her face. Her mind froze. The angry words vanished.

It was just a fleeting gesture, but one she felt right down to the bottoms of her soles. I'm too old to play games, Stacey. You're breathtakingly beautiful. I ache for you." His eyes darkened, his voice turned gravelly. He dropped his hand. "But I get the message. You're not interested. If you ever change your mind, though, let me know. We've tried avoiding each other..."

She opened her mouth to disagree, but he put a finger on her lips, effectively making it impossible to form thoughts, let alone say a single word.

"You've been avoiding me. And I've tried to stay out of your way. It's not working. I still think about you all the damn time. Maybe we should try something different. I want you even more now than I did when I first laid eyes on you in the dojo. And don't even try to tell me you don't remember that moment. You reacted to me as well. I noticed. I notice everything about you." With a final touch to her arm, he walked away.

For the rest of the evening, Stacey smiled and nodded and tried her level best to concentrate on what was being said around her, but it was difficult. Jason's words kept repeating over and over in her mind: "I ache for you" and "I want you even more than I did when I first laid eyes on you."

She'd been attending the self-defense classes at Blake

Davison's dojo when she'd first seen him. Blake had sent a message to all his students he'd be away for a couple of weeks but that the classes would continue. What she hadn't expected was that the replacement teacher would heat her blood, sending her heart spinning the moment she saw him.

So yeah, he was right—she remembered the precise moment their eyes had met.

The class had been a disaster. She'd been so rattled, that doing even the simplest of movements had been beyond her. It had been the last time she'd visited the dojo. What she hadn't known was that he'd also felt something at the time.

How was she supposed to carry on after those words as if nothing had happened? The embers glowing inside her ever since she'd first seen him had burst into flames, threatening to burn her alive after hearing those very explicit words.

At some point in the evening, she motioned to Lindsay she was leaving. She was so hot, even after she'd taken off the light sweater she'd put on under her coat. She had to get some air. She needed to cool down.

Outside, she inhaled the cold October air gratefully as she hurried to the parking spot behind the Suds Stop, glancing around her as she moved. As she neared her car, she heard footsteps behind her. With her keys in her hand, she turned around quickly.

She recognized the broad shoulders immediately. Jason.

"You frightened me," she scolded.

Jason put out his hand to soothe her. "I'm sorry. I didn't mean to do that, but Alisson is usually safe. Well, except for crazy ex-boyfriends like the one Lindsay had."

Stacey crossed her arms. "I you've grown up in South Africa like I have, you're always alert."

"Is that why you've relocated to Montana? You didn't

feel safe?"

"What is this? Twenty questions?" she asked, clearly irritated.

"No, this is what is called a normal conversation."

Combing her hair out of her face, she looked him in the eye. "What do you want, Jason?"

"I think I was pretty clear about that."

Angling her head, she smiled. "You do know what you're...okay, I'll admit, it's not just you. You do know what *we're* feeling is just biology, right?"

"Really?"

"Oh, yes. You should do an internet search on the topic—very enlightening. Our dopamine and norepinephrine levels are high at the moment because...well, because for some or other reason we're...we're attracted to one another. But it'll pass. It always does," she gestured with her hand, lifting her chin. "There is scientific proof that it does. Quite a few experiments confirm the same results."

Exasperated, he stared at her. Here he was, just about bursting out of his skin for wanting her, and she coolly told him what he was feeling was "just" biology?

"Tell you what," he said, equally coolly, and put his hands on her hips. "Why don't we take the experiment a little further?"

She immediately pulled his hands away from her hips but didn't drop them. "What do you mean?"

"Let's kiss. Maybe we won't feel a thing," he said as he bent his head slowly, giving her a chance to back away if she'd wanted to. He was near enough to catch her soft gasp. The slight tremor in her hands echoed in his heart. "Maybe you're right," he continued as his mouth lightly touched her ear. "Maybe this burning in my belly can be explained away by biology."

This time he was expecting the gasp, and gently catching her lips in a kiss, he swallowed the sound. He only lingered for a few seconds before he lifted his head.

Their mouths mere millimeters apart. "What do you think?" he murmured.

In the dim light of the streetlights her eyes were nearly black. "About...about what?" Her gaze was fixed on his lips, it took just about all his willpower not to simply pick her up and carry her to his truck.

He couldn't help smiling. "About what just happened. The kiss?"

With a soft mutter, she dropped her hands and turned toward her car. "If that's your idea of a kiss, it's no wonder you're still single," she threw over her shoulder.

He reached her car seconds before she did. "Wanna show me?"

"Go home, Jason, I'm not in the mood for playing games."

"I was hoping we could test your theory, but if you're too chicken..."

Her hands had slipped around his neck before he could blink. "You wanna kiss? Let me show you how it's done." Lifting her on her toes, she kissed him.

One minute he was still amused, but then soft, warm lips covered his and he forgot to breathe. His blood rushed through his body, extinguishing every other sound around them. Her unique scent, her soft curves fitting perfectly against his body, the soft sounds she made in her throat, sent his senses into overdrive and nearly brought him to his knees.

And then she was gone. Her car door slammed shut and she was driving away before he could catch his next breath.

Exhaling slowly, he stared after her. Damn, the woman was driving him crazy. It might be biology, but it was also a whole lot more.

Question was, how was he going to persuade the skittish Ms. Lawrence that their best course of action was to spend time together until this craziness had run its course? He absolutely agreed with her that it wouldn't last, but instead of lusting after one another, they might as well have fun while waiting for the fire to burn out.

Turning away, he walked toward his truck. It was no use going back inside the bar. The blonde waitress had signaled her willingness to go home with him later, but after kissing Stacey, he couldn't bear the thought of touching any other woman.

His phone bleeped; it was a text from Eleanor. Minutes later, he was still chuckling as he started his truck. It took a few tries but after a few hiccups, Maggie purred to life and he was able to drive away from the parking lot. He had to see Stacey tomorrow to have his picture taken, Eleanor had texted.

The last thing he wanted to do was to make a fool of himself by taking part in a bachelor's auction, but if it was giving him a chance to see more of the elusive Stacey Lawrence, he was happy to oblige.

ELSA WINCKLER

CHAPTER 3

By nine o'clock Saturday morning, Stacey had an outline for the poster Eleanor wanted, and was waiting in her shop for the bachelors to arrive to have their pictures taken.

She should expect them at ten, according to the text she'd received from Eleanor late last night. After tossing and turning for about an hour, she'd given up trying to sleep and had begun to work on the poster. It would help her to focus on something else besides Jason-freaking-Coleman, she'd thought, but even working straight through the night hadn't kept her from remembering what had happened between them in the parking lot.

All she could think about was the kiss. Well, okay, there were two kisses, but the one she'd initiated was the one keeping her all hot and bothered. She'd put her arms around his neck, lifted herself on her toes, and locked lips with him. It didn't last very long—at least she didn't think it had—but she remembered every single, sensory moment: his lips just about burning hers, his warm breath on her cheek, his toned shoulder muscles moving below her fingers, his firm body close to hers, the sure sign of his desire throbbing against her thighs.

Grabbing a piece of paper lying on the counter, she fanned herself in a vain attempt to cool down.

What had she been thinking? In the bright light of day, it was so obvious what she should've done—shoved him away when he'd first put his hands on her butt last night... She couldn't even blame a glass of wine. She was stone-cold sober. Oh, damn it, this wasn't helping.

Opening one of the cupboards in her office, she took out her camera. She was no professional photographer, but every now and again someone would ask her to take pictures at a wedding, for small parties or for family, pregnancy, or engagement shoots. Bachelors she hadn't photographed before—it was a whole different vibe.

The door opened and Billie rushed in, all smiles. "I was so happy to get your text this morning about the shoot today. Do you know who the bachelors are? Oh, I do hope Stone Warner is one of them. I'll bid on him any day."

Stacey smiled. It was impossible not to be swept up by Billie's enthusiasm for life and for single, young men in particular. "Thanks so much for coming in today, I appreciate it. I'm not quite sure exactly what Eleanor had in mind—"

The bell above the door rang and Eleanor burst into the shop, taking off her coat as she strode in. She was wearing a shocking pink oversized shirt paired with jeans and boots. No twin set and pearls for Eleanor. "Stacey, Billie!" She smiled when she saw them. "Oh, sweetheart, I'm so glad you're willing to take the pictures today," she said, grabbing Stacey's hand.

"I've rounded up as many bachelors as I could yesterday. Some needed more persuasion than others." Eleanor winked. "I'm hoping for at least one more, but I'm happy to report we have nine very attractive men for the auction. I've emailed all their phone numbers to you, Stacey, so that you can ask them to choose which picture we may use. I've met with other members of the committee for an early breakfast this morning and we decided there should be a bachelor menu, you know, in a booklet maybe, with a photo and a brief paragraph about each of the hunky guys, to hand out to the single ladies. And you won't mind doing that for us as well, do you, Stacey?" Out of breath, Eleanor finally inhaled. "I'm so excited!"

Her head reeling, Stacey couldn't help smiling. It was impossible to stay mad at the older woman. "You have been busy."

"And I have one more favor to ask," Eleanor mentioned tentatively, looking at Stacey. "But please say no if you can't do it. The whole evening is for the kids of this town who don't have it easy, but of course we'll understand if you have other plans. I was hoping you and Billie here will be there to help hand out the brochures at the doors? Tom McNeally, the high school football coach, has agreed to do the auctioning. Millie Jones will do the catering and Tod and Larry from the Suds Stop will run a cash bar. What have I forgotten?"

"Of course, we'll hand out the bachelor menus." Billie smiled. "I wouldn't miss the auction for the world."

"It would of course make more sense to have the information about each bachelor displayed on a screen," Stacey added.

"Ooh, I like that idea," Eleanor said. "But I still think everyone attending should have something in their hand with all the info as well." She frowned. "And where do we find another bachelor? I've wracked my brain trying to think of one more guy, but I haven't been able to pin down one more. Maybe I should try and find someone slightly older? What do you think? There are a number of…well, more mature ladies that would love to bid on someone more their age, don't you think? Problem is, he won't be here today to have his picture taken… Oh, I don't know. Probably a silly thought."

"I think it's a great idea," Stacey said. "What I could do is to just leave a silhouette for bachelor number ten,"

Stacey said. "Maybe create a bit of mystery that way."

Eleanor nodded slowly. "I like that idea. Oh, I knew you'd be able to help with this whole thing."

Behind Billie, the door to the shop opened again and the next moment the waiting area was filled with men, most of them clearly uncomfortable, but all were smiling.

Billie beamed. "Stone is here," she muttered softly.

The testosterone levels in the small room rose within seconds. Jason towered over all the men and above their heads, Stacey met his eyes. Her heart missed a beat and turning around quickly, she picked up her camera. The simple action took longer than usual. She was shaking. *Oh, my, the light in his eyes...*

Eleanor clapped her hands to silence everyone. "Welcome, and thank you all for being here. Stacey—I know you haven't had much time to think about this, but what did you have in mind for the photos?"

"Hi, everyone." Stacey tried her best not to look in Jason's direction. "I have a high chair ready in my studio. I thought that would work best. Please follow me."

Between jokes and gentle coaching from Eleanor, she managed to take photographs of all the men. Jason was last in line. She busied herself with the camera as he settled on to the chair.

"Ready?" she asked without looking up.

"Always."

She could practically hear the grin in his voice. Her finger was clicking away before she even realized it. All the men here today were attractive, well built, but there was just something about Jason Coleman that turned her insides to mush. All it took was one look from those blue eyes. He looked straight at the camera, directly into her heart. Her fingers were clumsy, her mind sluggish. Inhaling deeply, she forced herself to focus on what she was supposed to be doing—take pictures of Jason, not drool over him, for goodness' sake.

He moved as she instructed—where had the strange

huskiness in her voice came from?—but he never took his eyes off of her. When she'd finally finished and he got up from the chair, with a last heated gaze in her direction, she was a shuddering mess.

"Perfect." Eleanor was beaming, clapping her hands. "Now for one last picture. If you really don't feel comfortable doing it, I'll understand, but remember it's supposed to be fun and it is for a very good cause, after all. I was wondering if I could persuade you gentlemen to…uhm…well, unbutton your shirts for a final group picture?"

Gasping, Stacey nearly dropped the camera. "Eleanor…"

But among the shouts and groans of nine men, Eleanor didn't pay any attention to her.

Roger O'Connor, the local vet, was the first one to start unbuttoning his shirt. "I'm game. It *is* for a good cause," he said, and winked into the camera.

One by one the men opened their shirts and made an informal line in front of the camera. Jason ended up more or less in the middle, as if it wasn't difficult enough for Stacey to focus on anyone else but him.

At least one thing was now clear—her dreams hadn't done Jason's body any justice. What she could glimpse beneath the opened shirt had her salivating. Six-pack. Ripped. Muscled. Toned. All applied when describing his upper body. Her heart hammered away at an alarming rate. It took all of her control to focus on the task at hand.

By the time she was finished, she had a headache pounding away behind her eyes. The lack of sleep was finally catching up with her. Probably a lack of sex too. Quickly, she glanced at the other nine men. Eleanor had picked the sexiest bachelors in town, but none even came close to stirring her blood in the way Jason Coleman did. What was she going to do about him?

One by one the men began to leave, but though she called out goodbyes, Stacey made a point of keeping her eyes on her camera while looking through the photos.

At some point, Eleanor came over to her, fanning herself. "Well, I may be old, but not so old I can't appreciate a beautiful man." She gestured toward Stacey's camera. "Do you think you have enough pictures, Stacey?"

"Yes, I do. I'll look through them and send you the best ones. You let me know which ones you think we should put on the bachelor menus."

"And you'll be there to hand it out?" Eleanor pressed.

Shaking her head, Stacey smiled. "I won't stay, but I'll be there to hand out your menus."

Eleanor's eyes twinkled. "Well, that'll be a shame to miss out on the social event of the year. Thanks, Stacey—I so appreciate your help and time with this."

She turned toward the group of men. "If you could please let Stacey have your basic info, y you'll help me so much. Billie? Would you take down everyone's particulars for the bachelor menu, please?"

"What menu?" Jason asked.

"Oh, have I not mentioned that?" Eleanor asked innocently. "We'll have a menu of each of the bachelors and we need info from you, please. Just basic stuff like your height and weight, what you like, dislike, what you do, and so on. The ladies should know what they're bidding for, don't you think? That's why I wanted your mobile numbers. I've given them to Stacey here. She'll send you the final pictures and you get to choose which one we may use. Oh, and also send me your ideas for a dream date as soon as possible, please."

"A dream date?" someone asked. "Like having dinner?"

"Well, I hope you'll be a little bit more original." Eleanor chuckled. "The ladies who bid on you will expect something fun and interesting. You could ask Stacey and Billie here for ideas. Well, I think that's all. Oh, no, wait—one more thing—please wear a tux. The ladies would expect no less. Thanks, everyone, I'll see you in three weeks." And with a wave, Eleanor departed, ignoring the grunts and groans from the men.

"Follow me, please," Billie said to the bachelors, and motioned toward the waiting room area of the shop.

Relieved to be alone at last, Stacey grabbed her camera and walked toward her office. Rubbing her temple, she sat down behind her desk and pulled her laptop closer. She wanted to send the best pictures to Eleanor as soon as possible so she could work on deciding which ones to use for the menus.

Shaking her head, she linked her camera to her laptop. She'd agreed to do the posters and text everyone about the upcoming auction, but the list of things Eleanor wanted her to do kept growing.

Sighing, she tried to focus on picking out the best photos. She didn't really mind helping out. Eleanor has been so good to her when Stacey had first arrived in Alisson. She could never repay her for her help. If only Jason hadn't been part of this blasted auction.

The next picture she clicked on opened on her screen. A smiling Jason, his head angled to the one side, looked directly at her.

Her heart just about jumped out of her body and she closed her eyes. When she looked up, Jason—the real live one—was standing in front of her desk.

He was frowning. "You have a headache?"

"It's nothing really—"

"Do you have something to take for it?" he interrupted her as he walked around her desk to stand behind her.

She quickly shut her laptop.

Warm hands closed around her shoulders, gently massaging the tense muscles.

She swallowed the deep groan threatening to slip out. "I'll take some Tylenol when I get home."

"How long before you go home?"

"I have to finish this…"

"The photos?" he asked as his hand reached forward

and opened her laptop.

In silence, they both stared at his photo. His hands slid down her arms.

"I'll be right back," he said, heading for the door.

"Jason!" she called out after him, but he'd disappeared around the corner.

Gnashing her teeth, she opened her laptop again. Seriously, she didn't want to see him again. To have to look at his blasted pictures was bad enough, to have face the real-life Jason for a second time that day after she'd seen him half naked was...well, it was too much.

Quickly, she got up, picked up her laptop and camera, and walked toward the front door. A few bachelors were still hanging around Billie, so Stacey motioned she was leaving.

Minutes later, she was on her way home, her heart still pounding loudly in her ears. She'd moved countries, crossed a freaking ocean to find a place where she could live an uncomplicated life the way she wanted to.

Jason Coleman was threatening to become a big complication—she had to find a way to get him out of her system and out of her dreams.

CHAPTER 4

By the time Jason parked in front of Stacey's house fifteen minutes later, he was still ticked off. Damn it, he'd told the woman he'd be back. But did she wait for him? Oh, no, listening to anyone else was not something Ms. Lawrence did easily.

Grabbing the bag with tablets and the sandwich and coffee he'd bought for Stacey, he got out of his car. For a moment, he looked up at the snow-tipped mountains, his mind racing. What the hell was he doing here?

Sighing, he walked toward the front door of Stacey's house. He was here, because she was inside. She'd moved into this place when she'd arrived in town. Through the very active grapevine of Alisson, he'd heard she'd first rented the place and later bought it. Since then, she'd had construction builders here for a few months. The outside had been painted but apparently most of the work had been done inside.

He knocked. Silence. Her car was standing in the driveway, so she had to be home. He knocked again. Finally, he heard soft footsteps approaching the door. After long moments, the door finally opened. And he exhaled slowly. Damn, she was beautiful.

Dressed in sweatpants and an oversized top that left her one shoulder bare, her red hair carelessly gathered in a ponytail, she took his breath away. He had to say something but for a moment no coherent thought entered his mind. His brain had shut down completely and the only message his body was signaling was for him to drag her close and kiss her.

With superhuman effort, he managed to rein in the burning need to touch her. "I told you I'd be back. Why didn't you wait for me?"

Her eyes narrowed, and lifting her chin, she glared at him. "My mission in life is to never again be in a position where I have to do what other people tell me to do. I wanted to come home, so I did."

"Never again? Hard to imagine you've ever let anyone told you what to do."

"At the time I didn't have choice. Now I do. Why are you here, Jason?" Her voice was cool; it was clear she wanted him gone. He was about to turn away when he saw the fluttering pulse in her neck. Ah. So the lady was not as unaffected as she wanted him to think.

He lifted his hands. "I've brought you some Tylenol, a sandwich, and coffee. You probably haven't eaten anything this morning."

"Why?" Those blue eyes didn't give a thing away.

Exasperated, he swallowed a cussword. "Because for some or other damn strange reason I care about you and because I wanted to see you."

"Why? You saw me this morning?"

"Can we do the questions and answers inside, do you think?"

"Not a good idea."

"Why?"

"You know why. We'll end up kissing and…"

Grinning, he stepped closer. "Don't you like kissing me?"

Her eyes narrowed. "Look, Jason, you're a nice guy and

you're hot, and yes, damn it, I like your kisses, way too much for my peace of mind. But I'm not ever getting married and I definitely don't want babies. You deserve a woman who can give you all of those things and more. I wish you well, I truly do, but…"

With his gaze on her, he entered the house and closed the door behind him. "And you think you can tell me that, and expect me to turn around and go?"

"Yes…what…what are you doing?"

He put the items he'd bought down on a table near the door and pushed his hands into the pockets of his jeans. "I've told you."

"I'll repeat—I'm not ever getting married and I don't want babies."

"I haven't asked you to marry me," he stated slowly. "I'm not interested in anything permanent, either. But as I've told you in the bar, avoiding each other doesn't seem to lower those chemical levels you spoke about…"

"Dopamine and norepinephrine," she said primly. "Give it time, it'll happen…" Her damn chin was still tilted upward, so he bent down and silenced her with a kiss.

His hands were still in the pockets of his jeans. To take them out would unleash something he wouldn't be able to back away from.

Her lips softened. He welcomed her silent gasp, allowing his tongue to slide right through to where he could meet hers. Petals. Satin. Camellias.

Within seconds, all the blood in his body had moved down south. He ached for her, his body throbbing with need. Using all of his control, he lifted his head and stepped away from her. "I have a different solution to our mutual problem—you let me know when you're ready to listen to it." He couldn't resist touching her cheek. "Drink something for that headache and eat your sandwich."

His legs not quite steady, he left quickly. The woman was driving him insane. He needed to do something with all this pent-up energy. A long run before he hit the gym would hopefully help him to focus on something else besides the delectable Ms. Lawrence.

He started talking to his truck even before he'd reached it. "Not today, okay?"

And as if the truck understood his pleas, she started the first time. He really should take his new truck if he had to drive out as far as town.

Only when Stacey couldn't hear the engine of Jason's truck any longer, did she exhale. By this time, she was literally seeing stars and had to sit down quickly. Leaning forward in her chair, she tried to catch her breath.

Her body was on fire, her heart was kicking against her ribs, and her blood was roaring through her veins. Biology, she knew that. All could be explained away, but how was she supposed to survive the intense heat of this particular fire? She had been so close to grabbing his shirt and kissing him again—what was the matter with her?

Fanning herself, she got up and for the first time noticed the items he'd left on the table next to the front door. Tylenol for her headache, a coffee, and a sandwich.

Her tummy growled. How had he known she hadn't eaten all day? It was impossible not to like him, but she couldn't even allow herself to do that.

Minutes later, while swallowing the pill, she grimaced. So why was she standing alone in her kitchen, grinning like an idiot?

Taking the cup of coffee and sandwich with her, she quickly walked to the room in her house she used as an office. She had to finish these freaking photos, send them away so that she could carry on with the rest of her life.

Giving herself a stern lecture to focus, she opened her laptop. The first set of photos she clicked on, was of course, Jason's. Seriously. She'd taken fifteen pictures of him and there wasn't one in which he didn't look mouthwateringly sexy.

She quickly texted him the first five photos, asking him to choose one. One by one she worked through the photos of the other bachelors. All were attractive men, but not one of affected her hormones the way one look at Jason's pictures did.

Finally, she got to the last photograph, the one where the men had unbuttoned their shirts. She still couldn't believe Eleanor had asked them to do it. Chuckling, she scrolled through all her attempts with this picture. Brooke and Logan would probably have a fit when they heard what their mother had done, and the gossip mill would have a field day.

When she reached the very last picture of the group, her hand froze. Instead of a picture of the whole group, the camera had somehow zoomed in on Jason, capturing only him, the tantalizing glimpse his very sexy body beneath his shirt, the center point of the camera shot.

Muttering, she dropped her head in her hands. Surely, *she* hadn't done that? But when she looked up again, there he still was, smiling directly at her with his baby blues, glimpses of his ripped body sending her heart into overdrive. She exhaled slowly. There wasn't anybody else to blame for this picture but herself.

This one she had to delete as quickly as possible. With shaking fingers, she tried to press delete but her hand simply refused to obey the command from her brain. *Delete the damn thing.*

Scolding herself, she pressed a few buttons. A fluke, that was all it was. Finally, she chose the best group photos and sent them to Eleanor before she jumped up.

She was going for a walk. Hopefully, the cold air would clear her head and brought down her body temperature. When she got back, she would finish the posters so she could focus on her other work and put the whole freaking bachelor auction and Jason Coleman's sexy body behind her.

Jason was warming up before his run when his watch bleeped. It was a text from an unknown number, but he recognized who it was from instantly.

Let me know which one you prefer. S

He took out his phone. Six photos were attached. Quickly he glanced through them. At the last photo, he did a double take. When did she take this one? He'd only unbuttoned his shirt while she was taking the group photo, when did she take this one?

His mind went over photo shoot of the morning. The only explanation for this picture was that Stacey had zoomed in on just him while she was taking the group photo, or that she'd specifically cropped the rest of the fellas out.

Grinning, he dropped his arm and started his run. He couldn't care a damn which picture she chose; the whole thing was ridiculous anyway. If it hadn't been for the kids of this town, he would never have agreed to it. And of course, if it had been anyone else besides Eleanor asking, not even a good cause would've convinced him to take part. But he liked the older woman. She'd always been very nice to him, even if she liked to meddle.

Stacey Lawrence's presence at that moment when Eleanor had talked to him was part of the reason why he'd let himself be bamboozled into the whole thing. He was unable to focus on anything else when the red head was around.

He lengthened his strides, pushed himself to go faster and faster. The woman was in his thoughts, his blood, his dreams. Why the hell couldn't he just accept she wasn't interested?

Slowing down, he turned into the next street.

Because he'd kissed her, because he'd seen the pulse fluttering in her neck, he'd heard her gasping, seen the way her body reacted to his. Something happened when the two of them were together, whether she wanted to acknowledge it or not.

He looked up. Damn it to hell. He'd gone for a run to get her out of his mind but there she was walking toward him. Her head was bent down, earphones covering her ears, her gaze fixed on the ground in front of her, and she was moving quickly.

As she neared the corner, she looked up and saw him. Out of breath, hands on hips, she slowed down and stared at him as if she couldn't believe her eyes.

"So what's your excuse for being outside in the cold?" he asked.

She moved her earphones only slightly away from her ears. "I've finished working and wanted some fresh air."

"How's the headache?"

"Better, thanks." She moved to put her earphones back, but he touched her hand before he realized what he was doing.

"Interesting six photos you sent me," he said, watching her carefully.

She frowned. "Six? I only sent you five…" Her gaze dropped to his hand as he took out his phone.

He opened her text. "See? Six. And for the life of me, I can't remember when you took this one?"

Her face flaming, she glared at him. "Neither do I! I…I don't know how that happened. I've deleted it, don't worry. I have no idea how I ended up texting it to you."

For long moments they stared at each other. "A picture is a thousand words, they say," he murmured.

"I don't…I haven't… Please just delete it and forget I've sent it."

"Tell you what. Have dinner with me? At the bar. Not a date," he said quickly as she opened her mouth. "As friends working on a project together. You can help me choose which picture, and we can talk about why you've sent me this photo. And we can talk about a solution."

"What solution?"

"To the fact that there is something between us. That

you think about me. You can't deny it."

"Dating is not a good idea."

Swallowing a grin, he cleared his throat. "We're in a bar. With other people. I think we'll be able to keep our hands to ourselves for an hour or two. Well, I don't know about you, but I should be able to."

"Jason, seriously…"

"I'm asking you to have dinner with me, Stacey, not have my babies. I'll pick you up at seven."

Before she could answer, he turned away and began jogging again. When he'd reached the end of the street, he looked back. She was still standing where he'd left her. When she saw him watching her, she stomped away, chin in the air.

He was still chuckling when he returned to his house an hour later.

CHAPTER 5

Stacey was just taking out her phone to send Jason a message—to say she wasn't going anywhere with him—when her doorbell chimed. It was half past six. She hadn't quite finished dressing, and most of her wardrobe was lying on her bed.

She been in a state since she'd met him on the street and had tried to think how it was possible that she'd send him the picture where his shirt had been unbuttoned.

Was it a subconscious thing?

The bell rang again. Jason was supposed to arrive at seven, so it was probably one of the neighbors at her front door. After Jason's visit earlier that day, she'd been expecting one or two of them to pop over to ask her some or other seemingly innocent question in order to get to the real reason for their visit: why had Jason Coleman been to her house?

As she quickly walked toward the door, she looked down at herself. After long deliberation, she'd finally settled for her favorite jeans and a yellow top she felt good in. The soft knit fitted snugly and left her shoulders bare. With it she wore thin gold chain she'd bought herself on the day she realized she actually had money.

However, she was getting back into her sweatpants after she'd gotten rid of the nosey neighbor.

Of course, she couldn't go to the bar with Jason, or anywhere else for that matter. If she wanted to get him out of her system, *not* seeing him was the better option. There was no other "solution,'" there was no need to have dinner to discuss it. Stay away from each other, no matter how long it took, and whatever crazy feeling there was would fade eventually.

The doorbell chimed again, and irritated, she rushed forward to open it. It wasn't any of her neighbors, though, but Jason standing on her doorstep, a box of chocolates in his hand.

"Jason, you're—"

"Early, I know. But I was ready and didn't want you to chicken out."

She narrowed her eyes. "I wasn't going to chicken out. I was merely going to send you message to say I don't think it's a good idea to have dinner when we…when we…"

"Can't keep our hands to ourselves?" he asked innocently.

"That's not what I was going to say!"

"This is for you." He handed her the box of chocolates. "The flower shop was closed."

"Thank you." She couldn't help smiling. "Chocolates are my kryptonite."

"Good to know. Shall we go?"

She shouldn't. Shouldn't go. She should send him away, but even as she opened her mouth, she knew that was not what she was going to say. "Come in. I'm not quite finished yet."

"I'll wait out here."

"Don't be silly. It's cold—"

"If I come in, we won't leave."

Her breath hitched somewhere in her throat. "You can't say stuff like that." She barely got the words out.

"Grab a coat as well, Stace. It's cold."

Turning around, she fled. The expression in his eyes was enough for those simmering embers to flare up again. This was such a bad idea.

Stace. Nobody had ever shortened her name before, or if they had, she didn't remember it. When Jason said it, though… Oh, my. She was in deep, deep trouble.

When she stepped outside, he was leaning against what looked like a brand-new truck.

"Fancy," she said as she moved toward the door.

"I prefer Maggie. She belonged to my grandpa. This one is more reliable, though," he said as he helped her inside. "Just don't say it out loud in front of her."

"She has a name, has she?" she asked, eyebrows raised.

"Of course," he insisted. "My grandma's name. My mother was also Margaret."

Returning the grin, she looked away. She liked this guy. Really, really liked him.

Oh, dear.

He and Stacey had just ordered dinner when a group of what looked like students burst into the bar. They were laughing and talking, all clearly in a good mood. It was Saturday night; the place was packed as it usually was over weekends, but visitors meant business and that was good for the town. Everybody greeted the newcomers with a smile or a wave.

Stacey had been sitting with her back toward the door and quickly looked over her shoulder. "It's going to become a lot louder." She smiled.

Jason lifted his beer. "To our first date."

She was shaking her head even before he'd finished talking. "It's not a date."

He shook his head. "Okay. To our first not-date."

Glaring at him, she took a sip of her glass of wine.

He leaned forward. "I like being with you, Stace, and I

don't see why we can't be together—date, not-date, whatever you want to call it—until the fire between us has run its course." He grinned. "I'm definitely not in the market for anything permanent, either. A woman telling me up front she's not interested in marriage and babies means I don't have to explain that. Bargain, as far as I'm concerned."

Her eyes narrowed ever so slightly. "I don't see how spending more time together would make a difference. After the auction, there's no reason for us to see each other. The craziness will eventually disappear."

"May I remind you, we've tried that, and it's not working. If anything, the need to touch you, to be with you, is way more intense than what it was a year ago."

Exhaling slowly, she looked away. He had to use every ounce of his willpower not to reach out and touch her.

"And if it doesn't disappear?" she asked.

"You're the expert on the subject. Didn't you say according to your research, it's only temporary?"

Nodding, she took another sip of her wine. A slight frown marred her forehead.

What the hell was her problem? "Look, if you're that unhappy about it—"

"Okay," she said.

But he was on a roll and didn't immediately catch what she was saying. "Forget about it. The idea is to enjoy each other but if…" Her words finally registered, and he stopped, subconsciously aware his mouth must still be open. "Okay?"

The corners of her mouth lifted ever so slightly upward. "Okay."

Grabbing the keys to his truck, he moved to stand up. "Let's go."

Instead of jumping up as he'd thought she would do, she crossed her arms, chin lifted. "I'm hungry. You promised me dinner."

Stunned, he stared at her. He was ready to explode, and

she wanted food? "You seriously want to eat right now?"

Her eyes were twinkling. "I do." She sounded cool and collected, but the pulse in her neck was beating frantically.

Shaking his head, he leaned back in his chair and exhaled slowly. "You do know I'm going to kiss you senseless once we leave the bar," he growled.

Intrigued, he watched as her cheeks turned pink.

Picking up her glass, she took a sip. "Don't say things like that!"

"You'll have to get used to it. Told you, I'm too old to play games."

"Jason…" she began, but a new voice interrupted her.

"Stacey?"

Frowning, Stacey turned her head to look at the young man standing next to their table.

"Do I know you?" she asked coolly.

"I'm Christopher, your cousin."

Stacey's eyes widened. "Christopher? Oh, my goodness, look at you! All grown up."

Touching her shoulder, he laughed. "I knew you were somewhere in the States but we didn't know where you were. I've missed you. The twins are still talking about you." For the first time, he looked in Jason's direction. "Sorry about the intrusion, but I haven't seen my cousin in what?" He looked back to where Stacey was still sitting. "I was twelve when you left. You were nineteen, if I remember correctly."

"Yes, you're right. So how have you been?"

He offered Jason his hand. "Christopher Warner, Stacey's cousin," he said, before turning back to Stacey. "I'm studying architecture at University of Cape Town and the hiking club planned a trip to hike the North Rim Trail in the Yellowstone River National Park. We're here until Monday morning. Can I buy you a coffee tomorrow? There are so many things I want to talk to you about." He glanced in Jason's direction before he continued. "I also want to…" shaking his head, he stared at Stacey. "I just never thought I'd see you again. I want to try and apologize for my mother and try and explain why—"

"Let's meet at the coffee shop in town tomorrow. Does eleven work?" Stacey interrupted him. "You can't miss it, there's just one."

"Sounds great. You look well, by the way." He smiled. With another backward glance, he walked to the bar where his friends were waiting.

Stacey's eyes followed her cousin, she was clearly rattled.

He leaned forward and touched her hand. "Stace? Are you okay?"

"Just stunned. I never thought I'd see him again. Jason, I'm sorry, but I...I want to go home."

"Tell you what." He handed her the keys. "Wait in the truck. I'll get the food to go. It should be ready by now." Even before he'd finished speaking, she was heading for the door.

Feeling faint, Stacey leaned against Jason's truck. She'd thought she'd put her past behind her, but after seeing her cousin, it was all coming back to her.

Of all the states in the USA, of all the towns in Montana, Christopher was here, in Alisson. The panicky feeling that she was trapped in a place where she didn't want to be, didn't belong, the feeling she'd lived with for seven long years, grabbed her around her throat.

"Stace, babe, are you okay?" Jason's soft voice spoke from behind her. A big, reassuring hand folded over her shoulder.

She nodded. "I'm fine. Seeing Christopher...has brought back some not-so-nice memories. Not him—he's always been a nice kid."

"Come on, we can eat at your house." Gently, he took her hand, opened the car door for her, and helped her inside.

She'd been so sure she'd processed the seven years she lived with her aunt, but everything was coming back. In the bigger picture, it probably hadn't been that bad. She'd had a roof over her head and there was food, but nothing in her previous life had prepared her for someone as spiteful and nasty as her aunt Penelope had been to her.

As Jason drove down the street toward her house, he took her hand in his. Fortunately, he didn't try and talk to her again.

At her front door, Jason took her key and opened the door. At any other time, she would've been miffed but her fingers were icy cold. There was no way she could have managed it herself.

He closed the door behind them. "Kitchen that way?" he asked.

She nodded, her mind in the past.

Frowning, he put the food down and walked toward her. "Talk to me, please?"

"I...there isn't much to tell, really. When I was twelve, I went to live with my aunt's family. Seeing Christopher tonight brought back memories of that time."

"Stace, sweetheart, come here..." He picked her up. Cradling her against his broad chest, he walked toward the couch and sat down, still holding her close.

She couldn't remember ever being picked up this way. He was warm and solid, making her feel safe, just what she needed at the moment. It couldn't hurt to lean against him, just for a moment. Pressing her face against his chest, she inhaled his maleness, his strength.

"I've got you, Stace, I've got you," he whispered as his hands slid up and down her back.

Tears clogged up her throat. All efforts to try and keep them from falling were in vain. And once the first tear rolled down her cheek, there was no holding back. Seven years of pent-up anger, seven years of feeling helpless and afraid, had finally caught up with her and she did something she hadn't done since she'd left South Africa—

she cried.

CHAPTER 6

Completely out of his depth, Jason tightened his grip on Stacey. Bad guys, danger, explosive situations—those he could handle. Tears and comforting someone, not so much. He had no idea what to say or do to help her.

What exactly had happened in Stacey's past he didn't know but whatever it was, it was clearly still affecting her. Why would her cousin want to apologize for his mother?

"You should come and visit me on the ranch," he began, not even sure whether she could hear him, but maybe his voice would calm her down. It worked for horses. "My grandpa used to have a ranch in Wyoming and Mom sent me there over holidays. Sometimes she joined us, but she had to work, so it was usually only Grandpa and me. My dad was never in the picture. Apparently, he left when I was a baby. When Grandpa passed away, the ranch was sold. I missed the wide, open spaces, the quiet, the animals, and promised myself I'd buy a ranch as soon as I could. When mom passed away, I discovered she'd invested Grandpa's money he got from selling his ranch, and left it all to me. So I started looking for land. That's partly the reason how I ended up in Alisson."

As he talked, he kept up the rhythmic stroking of her back. After a long while, the shudders stopped and eventually so did the shivering. Quietly, she lay in his arms, her face still pressed against his chest. He continued talking about his land, described the house to her, the plans he had to change it.

When he eventually ran out of things to say, he looked down at her. There was still a shimmer of tears on her long eyelashes, but at least she'd stopped crying. Exhaling slowly, he tucked the strands of hair that had fallen over her face behind her ear.

Damn, she was beautiful. This was the first time he'd allowed himself to just look at her. In this up close and very personal space, she was even more gorgeous than he'd realized. Slowly he slid his gaze over her face: perfectly formed eyebrows, high cheekbones, tiny freckles sprinkled over the top of her nose, soft, kissable mouth, stubborn chin.

She was tall, slender, and didn't weigh that much. He had no trouble picking her up in his arms a while ago. But she was so brave. Moving countries, setting up her own shop, making a success of a business in a small town—all of that took courage and grit. She'd done all of that while obviously carrying a huge chunk of hurt around.

Would her past be the reason she never wanted to marry or have babies?

What the hell was he thinking about? *I don't want those things either, remember?*

She moved restlessly against him, and his body responded. Cussing under his breath, he tried a different position, but everywhere he turned, soft, womanly curves followed.

Blue eyes looked up at him.

"You okay?" What a stupid question, but he wasn't sure what else to say.

"I will be," she said. "Sorry I cried all over you. I can't remember when last I sobbed like that."

"Wanna talk about it?"

She was quiet for a long time. "I've never talked about it before. I don't like to be reminded of the time I've lived with my aunt's family. It's of course possible my mind has made it into a much worse experience than it actually was. Memory, I've discovered, is a strange thing."

While she talked, her hand moved slowly over his chest, making it even more difficult to stay still. She was vulnerable and he didn't want to take advantage of that. "Do you have wine in this house?" he asked.

"Yes, I come from a wine region in South Africa. I always have wine."

"A girl after my own heart." The words just slipped out. Only afterward did he realize what he'd said.

"Do we have to move?" she asked, still lying against his chest.

He exhaled slowly. "Two reasons—one, I'm really hungry and two, if we sit like this for much longer, I'm going to kiss you and I'm not going to stop until we're both naked."

Those deep blue eyes turned up to stare at him. "So what's stopping you?"

Cussing under his breath, he quickly got up and put her down gently. "The fact that you've been crying. When you and I make love, Stace, I want you with me all the way, eyes wide open. I want you to know exactly what you're doing." Turning away, he walked toward her kitchen. "Where do I find glasses?"

Despite her chaotic state of mind, delicious shivers tingled down Stacey's spine. She inhaled deeply. *When* they made love, he'd said, as if it already was a fait accompli.

Minutes ago, she'd been ready to forget about everything else and give herself over to his lovemaking. He'd be able to silence her chaotic thoughts, make her forget the past, she thought. But again, he'd surprised her.

He was opening cupboards, taking out glasses, plates, and cutlery. For a moment, her eyes roamed over him— broad shoulders, firm butt, arm muscles rippling... Oh, my goodness, she was just about drooling.

She quickly moved toward the cupboard. "The wine is over here. What do you prefer?"

"I'm not really picky. You choose," he offered, while popping their food into the microwave.

"That's no answer," she scolded. "If you want to spend time with me, you better learn about wine. I prefer a Shiraz, although I've been struggling to get any around here. Fortunately, my favorite cellar in South Africa delivers all over the world." She poured the wine, handed him a glass.

Leaning against the kitchen cupboard, he lifted his glass. "What do we drink to?"

"Friendship."

Shaking his head, he sighed. "You and I can never be just friends. Besides, I haven't forgotten you've agreed to my proposal that we spend more time together. You're not backing out, I hope?"

The microwave pinged, indicating their food was ready. Jason took it out and placed on the table. He pulled out a chair for her.

"I can get my own chair," she said as she sat down.

"I know. You're one of the most independent women I know. It's kinda sexy, even if it is intimidating." He sat down opposite her.

"An FBI agent, intimidated?"

"Ex-FBI. And yeah, you're a class act, Ms. Lawrence."

For a few minutes they ate in silence. She hadn't planned on telling him about her past, but somehow as she relaxed, her mouth opened and the words simply rushed out, as if they'd been waiting all the time for this particular moment.

"My parents were killed in a freak accident when I was twelve," she began. "We were holidaying in Hermanus, our favorite holiday destination in summer. The one moment, Mom and Dad were standing on the rocks and the next, a freak wave took them into the sea. Their bodies were found only much later."

Putting down his knife and fork, he took her hand. "It must've been devastating. I'm so sorry you had to go through that."

"My life changed overnight. My aunt—my mom's sister—Aunt Penelope took me in. I didn't even know I had an aunt. She and her husband, George, have three kids. Christopher was five at the time and the twins, Kevin and Penny, were two years old. Uncle George worked long hours and he was away on some or other business trip most of the time. To say she resented having to look after me is putting it mildly. I had to work for my keep, she used to tell me, and that meant looking after the twins after school and during holidays. When they were older, I began to babysit for the neighborhood." She grimaced. "Hence my no-babies rule. I swear I can feel my ovaries clutching my eggs every time I hear a baby cry. And it's not funny!" she added, when he burst out laughing.

"Sorry, but I don't think I'll ever get that particular image out of my head. Continue."

"I won't bore you with the details. Fast forward seven years. I discovered I was the sole heir to my grandmother's estate, my dad's mother, although Aunt Penelope kept this from me for a long time. When I realized I was free to do as I pleased, I stopped looking after babies, finished my studies, and then left South Africa as soon as I sorted out the admin. Dad was an American. I was born in New York before he and my mom moved to South Africa, so that made relocating much less complicated. For about four years, I literally visited every single state of the US of A, stayed in towns or cities for a while before I moved on. One night, a television show featured the quaint town of Alisson. I decided to move here and see if I liked it."

"And here we are." He smiled.

She nodded. "And here we are."

He was still holding her hand. "What you've told me is obviously the very short version of what you went through, and it's fine. I understand why you don't want to talk about bad memories, but as I've learned, you have to deal with it, otherwise your past will always have a hold over you."

She rolled her eyes. "Next thing you'll tell me I have to see a shrink."

"Well, that's what I did," he said quietly.

Surprised, she stared at him. "Really? Don't men just kick something and get things out of their system?"

He smiled. "Unfortunately, it doesn't work that way." He looked down at his wine. "In my line of work you get to see the very worst of life and of people. I had issues I needed to deal with when I quit. It took me a while to acknowledge I needed help, but I eventually realized that if I want to keep moving forward, I have to deal with stuff. I still get nightmares, but I know what to do now."

"That easy?"

"That hard. And I've never told a soul what I've just told you."

"See? We're friends," she said, trying to lighten the moment.

His blue eyes darkened. "Well, this friend still wants to kiss you senseless."

She put down her glass. "Jason...you're a really nice guy, but it won't work. I don't do relationships, I won't even know how. I appreciate your help tonight and for letting me cry all over you, but I just don't think I can do this. You're a great guy and you make me feel things I've never felt before, but this can never go anywhere. I'm sorry."

"You've agreed earlier tonight, remember?"

"I know but it won't be fair to you. You need to marry someone and raise babies on your ranch—you're clearly very happy there."

"So you actually heard my ramblings back there?" He smiled.

"You have a very soothing voice."

"It works on horses," he teased.

She nodded. "At first I didn't hear what you were saying but you speak about your ranch with so much passion, you're obviously very proud of it. I'm sorry about your mom...?

He nodded. "She passed away a while back. Cancer. It was at that time I decided to stop chasing bad guys and buy a ranch, as I've always wanted to."

"I'm sorry you've lost her. And I'm sorry about your dad."

He shrugged. "I never knew him. But he's the reason why I've decided marriage and babies are not for me. Leaving your wife and kid behind without a second thought? Then I'd rather not marry."

"I hardly know you, but from what I've seen, you'd never walk out on anyone, least of all your own child. Surely you know that?" she asked. "You're a great guy, Jason. You'd be a great husband and dad. Thank you for tonight, but I think it's best if we don't see each other again."

Cussing softly, he shoved back his chair and got up. "My feelings haven't changed because you're suddenly getting cold feet. If anything, I want you even more. But if that's your final answer, I'll go. You know where to find me if you change your mind."

She was still sitting at the table when his truck drove away. At the sound, those stupid tears were back.

CHAPTER 7

Sunday morning, just before eleven, Jason was sitting in his truck outside the coffee shop. What the hell was he doing here? Stacey had been very clear—there could never be anything between the two of them. But here he was, waiting to make sure she wouldn't be upset after she talked to her cousin. He'd never forgive himself if she left here upset and she had no one to turn to.

He'd hardly slept. What she'd told him about her past kept replaying over and over in his mind. He couldn't image the trauma she had to go through from living with loving parents to living in a house where she'd been abused. A whole night of thinking and dreaming about her had made that clear. Contrary to what she'd claimed, what had happened to her was abuse: there was no other word to describe telling a twelve-year-old girl to look after two babies, and withholding the news about her inheritance was a straight-up crime.

Stacey's car was already parked in front of the coffee shop. By now she was probably inside, waiting for her cousin.

A slap on the roof of his truck shook him out of his reverie. Blake stood there, a broad smile on his face. Jason rolled down his window.

"What are you doing here?" Blake asked.

"On my way to have coffee."

"Mind if I join you?" Blake asked, looking at the beat-up truck. "You sure this thing will get you back home?"

"Not if you talk to her like that." Jason frowned.

As Jason opened the door and got out, he noticed Christopher entering the coffee shop. "How come you're alone in town on a Sunday morning?"

"The number of diapers a one-month-old baby uses is staggering." Blake chuckled.

As they walked toward the coffee shop, Blake couldn't stop talking about his wife or his baby. "Can't wait to see her in the morning," Blake ended with a wink.

Jason shook his head as they entered the coffee shop. "If someone told me two years ago you'll be smiling this much, I wouldn't have believed it."

They sat down at the first table. Jason glanced over Blake's shoulder to where Stacey and Christopher were sitting. Her back was turned toward them and she hadn't seen them yet.

"So what or who has caught your attention..." Blake asked as he turned to look behind him. "Ah, I see. Eleanor has been trying for ages to get you and Stacey together, I know."

The waitress arrived and they ordered coffee.

"She the real reason you're here?" Blake asked.

Jason nodded. "It's complicated."

"If she's the one for you, it isn't really, you know? I've looked for so many reasons not to be with Lindsay but in the end, it was so simple. She lights up my life. But I have to warn you—you hurt Stacey and you'll have to deal with me. She doesn't have family around to look out for her."

"Yeah?" Jason tried to joke.

Blake was serious though. "I've seen you operate, remember? You don't stick around after a couple of dates."

"It's a moot point. She's not interested."

Fortunately, Blake changed the topic and by the time they'd finished their coffee, Stacey and Christopher were still talking. There was no reason to linger and when Blake got up to leave, Jason joined him.

Christopher was speaking about their past when the hair on Stacey's neck rose. She didn't have to turn her head around to know Jason was also in the coffee shop. Why was he here?

"As I said last night, I want to apologize for my mother." Shaking his head, he peered into his coffee mug. "What she did to you is unforgivable, I know. I only realized what she expected from you much later, when I was older. What I do remember, though, is the way she'd shout at you."

Grimacing, Stacey looked away. "I was probably difficult. I don't know…"

He grabbed her hands. "No, Stacey, you did nothing wrong. My mum was the one with the problem." He shook his head. "It took me a number of sessions with a psychologist to be able to say that. Did you know what happened between my mother and yours?"

Stacey shook her head. "I was only twelve at the time my parents died. I didn't even know that the Penelope my parents sometimes talked about was my aunt. Mom never told me anything about her."

He nodded. "If I understand my mother's ramblings correctly, she carried a torch for your dad ever since she met him. They were all students together. Apparently, Mom brought your dad home one Christmas, hoping he'd propose to her. Instead, he and your mom fell in love and got married. I don't think she ever forgave them, and she never got over that."

Stunned, Stacey stared at her cousin. "And then I was dumped on her. I didn't know that. At least now I understand why I didn't know about her until after my parents passed away."

"After you were gone, my mother had a complete breakdown. It was only then my dad discovered how she'd treated you. He was so seldom home and didn't even realize what was going on until after you left. Kevin and Penny kept crying for you, and Mom...well, she had no idea what to do. She was treated for depression for a while but never quite recovered. She...passed away a few years back."

Stacey struggled to breathe. She was ice cold. Somewhere in her mind she'd always had this picture of Aunt Penelope apologizing to her for what she'd put Stacey through. Now it would never happen, she would never be able to confront her aunt.

"Dad has remarried," Christopher was saying. "He's happy now and the twins are doing much better."

Reeling from everything she'd just heard, Stacey nodded. "That's good news. Are you okay? I'm so glad to hear you're studying. You've always been so bright."

"I'm fine." He gave her a lopsided grin. "Dad insisted we all see a psychologist after my mom's death. It made things easier. Anyway, I'm so glad I've run into you. We're leaving early tomorrow, but we're passing this way again on our way back to catch a plane from Bozeman. Would you mind if I stop by again?"

"Of course not. I appreciate you taking the time to see me."

"We're family. I hope we'll stay in contact when I'm back in South Africa?"

"I'd like that." Stacey smiled.

"Great. Coffee is on me. Let me pay, and I'll walk you out."

Outside the coffee shop, Jason turned his head. Stacey and her cousin were still talking.

Blake slapped him on the shoulder. "If you're serious about her, tell her how you feel."

Startled, Jason looked at his friend. "It's not the same as you and Lindsay...I hardly know her. It's just..."

Blake shook his head. "Take it from me, life is short. Decide what you want and go for it."

"She's very adamant about not ever getting married or having babies. Her excuse for why she doesn't date."

"Well..."

"Jason! Blake!" someone called out.

Cussing under his breath, Blake made a hasty retreat. "You're on your own, pal. Surely you can handle Sandy Rivers by yourself? I'm a happily married man." With a wave of his hand, he hurried toward his truck.

By this time Sandy had reached Jason and she grabbed his arm. "Oh, it's so nice to see you! Where did Blake go? What about a coffee?"

"Uhm...we just had coffee, thanks. I...I have another appointment..."

"Oh, nonsense," she said, and clinging to his arm, she literally dragged him back into the coffee shop.

As they entered, Stacey and Christopher were just on their way out. Stacey's eyes zoomed in on Sandy's arm curved around his. He tried to extract himself, but Sandy wouldn't budge.

"Hi, Stacey!" Sandy greeted her.

"Sandy, Jason." She nodded and walked quickly past them.

Christopher also nodded in his direction before he followed Stacey outside.

Jason finally managed to extract his arm from Sandy's grip. "I'm sorry, Sandy, I really have to go." Without looking back, he rushed out after Stacey.

"Seriously?" Sandy called out after him.

He ignored her. Sandy was lonely, he got that, but man, ever since she'd joined the classes at the dojo, she'd been making life difficult. Up 'til now, he'd succeeded in not being rude, but maybe that would be the only way to make her understand he wasn't interested.

He caught Stacey as she got into her car. "Stacey, wait."

"What do you want, Jason?"

"Are you okay?"

"Why do you care? You seemed to have moved on rather quickly, and I'm glad. You should find someone who you can share your life and ranch with."

"Damn it, you know what Sandy is like. She flirts with everyone."

"She had her hands all over you."

"I didn't touch her."

"You don't have to explain anything to me, remember?"

"I'm here because I want to make sure you're okay."

She closed the door, rolled down the window. "I'm not your problem, Jason, but I'm okay. Thank you for asking. I...I have to go."

He bent down and kissed her. For a moment, her mouth softened under his before she pulled back and quickly looked away. But not before he'd seen the shimmer of tears in her eyes.

"You're crying!"

"I'm fine. Goodbye, Jason."

Stacey quickly drove home. If Jason followed her now... But a quick glance in her rearview mirror made her relax. He was still standing where she'd left him, staring after her.

Listening to her cousin and keeping her emotions in check had been bad enough. Seeing Jason with another woman's hands all over him was devastating.

Fortunately, she didn't have any commitments that day. She needed to be alone to process everything. Of course, Jason would move on. *You told him to, remember?*

Sighing, she parked next to her house and dropped her

head in her hands for a moment, trying to find her equilibrium.

Christopher had told her about his mom. Aunt Penelope had had depression. Was that the reason she'd been so nasty? Or had she been so bitter about the man of her dreams marrying someone else that she'd held his child responsible?

With a sigh, she got out of the car.

She'd dreamed of the day she could confront her aunt and tell her exactly how she'd made her feel, how frightened and scared she'd been, how helpless she'd felt. If she could do that, maybe she'd be able to move forward, she'd thought. Her aunt was dead, though. There would never be a chance to voice how much she'd been hurt.

Anger built up, fast and insistent. What could she kick or throw? And then she remembered what Jason had shared: *you had to deal with bad memories from your past, otherwise your past will always have a hold over you.*

Groaning, she sat down on the nearest chair. For so long, her resentment toward her aunt had had been a part of her. How did she change that? How did she let go of the anger? The hurt?

Jason had seen "someone," he'd confessed. And so had Christopher, and the twins, apparently. Could she be that brave?

Sighing, she got up. Her brain was too tired to think. Her house needed cleaning. At least that would keep her thoughts at bay for a while.

CHAPTER 8

Monday morning was busy. Not only had Billie phoned to say she was not feeling well, just about everyone in town had found some or other reason to visit Stacey's shop. The real reason for the visits soon became clear, though. Apparently, the town gossip mill had been hard at work.

By late morning it was obvious everyone in town knew that one: she and Jason had had dinner at the bar, two: she and a stranger had had coffee on Sunday morning, and three: Sandy Rivers had had her hands all over Jason.

And of course, everybody wanted to talk about the group photo of the bachelors, the one Eleanor wanted on the posters. The most popular question? Where was the picture where the bachelors were completely shirtless? Everyone seemed convinced she'd taken such a photograph.

When the bell above the door rang again, she had to gnash her teeth. Surely, there couldn't be a soul left in town who hadn't been here to ask about the rumors or talk about the posters.

She recognized the older man who'd entered immediately. Guy Richard was a well-respected attorney in town. She'd met him at Brooke and Gavin's wedding. He'd been Eleanor's escort for the occasion, something that had kept the gossipers busy for weeks afterward.

"Good morning, Mr. Richard." She smiled. "What can I do for you?"

Looking slightly uncomfortable, he stepped closer to the counter. "Good morning, Stacey. Please call me Guy. I…uhm…believe you are still looking for a bachelor for the auction?"

Stacey's eyes widened. "We are indeed."

Shifting from one foot to the other, he grimaced. "Before we continue, this conversation is strictly between you and me?"

Keeping a straight face was fast becoming very difficult. "Of course, although the bachelors have to make an appearance on the night of the auction."

"I'll do that, but I don't want anyone to know before the time. And I'm not having my picture taken."

"Whatever you say. I understand. We have decided to go with just a silhouette for bachelor number ten, anyway. Let me show you." As she opened one of the posters lying on the counter, she sneaked another peek at the new bachelor. "So has Eleanor…?"

"No, I haven't seen or talked to her since Brooke's wedding. Apparently, she's very busy. Which is why I'm here. We're not getting any younger. Maybe this way I'll get her attention."

Biting her cheeks, Stacey showed him the final poster. The faces of nine bachelors were arranged against the background of the mountains surrounding Alisson. For bachelor number ten, there was only the silhouette of a face.

Such a pity she couldn't repeat any of this to anyone.

"That would work. What do you expect of me on night of the auction?" Guy asked primly.

"Well, Eleanor is the one organizing the event, but as far as I know, you should wear a tux and show up on time. Oh, and give us an idea of the kind of date you're going to take with the woman who would win you."

"And no one else would know about this before the time?"

"I promise." Stacey nodded.

Lindsay strolled into the dojo late Monday afternoon, baby in her arms. When she saw Jason, she changed direction and walked over to where he was waiting for the next class.

"Hi, Jason. I've been shopping this morning and goodness me, you have the town abuzz. Apparently, you've had an interesting and busy weekend.

Groaning, he shook his head. "Seriously? More people should come for classes. They obviously don't have enough to do. How's baby?" he asked, peering down at the small face.

"She's fine. We don't sleep much, but we've learned that's part and parcel of having babies. You want to hold her?"

"I…I don't know. Won't I hurt her?"

"Of course you won't." Lindsay chuckled and proceeded to put the baby in his arms. "Keep your hand underneath her head, like this, and hold her close to your body."

Gingerly, he took the small bundle from her mother. Just then, the baby's eyes opened and she stared straight up at him. "Look at that," he murmured. "You're a cutie, aren't you?"

"I hear you have quite a way with the ladies," Lindsay continued. "Not only did you wine and dine Stacey Saturday night, but your car was also seen parked outside her house for quite a while. But then—and this baffles everyone—the next morning, you had coffee with Sandy Rivers."

Grimacing, Jason handed the baby back to her mother. "Yes, Stacey and I went for dinner. We finished eating it at her house, though. She was upset..." The minute the words left his mouth, he knew he'd said too much.

Lindsay frowned. "Why was she upset? Does it have anything to do with the young man she had coffee with yesterday morning?"

"You'll have to ask her about it."

"I don't think I've ever heard her talk about her past. But what I still don't know is why go out with her one night and the next morning you're having coffee with Sandy Rivers?"

"I didn't have coffee with Sandy. She grabbed my arm, but I didn't go into the coffee shop with her. And Stacey? Well, she's not interested in dating."

"Oh, well. I really thought you'd be the guy to change her mind. There's still the bachelor auction, though, isn't there? Anything can happen in three weeks!" And with a grin, she turned around and went looking for her husband.

Just then, the first few students for his next class arrived. According to the sly glances he was getting, everybody knew about the weekend.

Damn it to hell. It was going to be a long day.

When Stacey's phone rang on Wednesday, just before lunch, she swallowed a groan. It was Eleanor. Again. The older woman had been phoning daily. Seriously, it wasn't as if she was getting paid to help with the auction.

Grimacing, Stacey answered, trying to sound as cheerful as possible. "Eleanor, hi. No, Billie is still ill and I haven't been able to get the posters to the dojo. Lindsay's assistant has kindly fetched a poster for their window and I was able to get one to the pharmacy over lunch yesterday, but..."

"Oh, I know you'd find a way. Thanks so much, Stacey. You're a star. If you could find time over lunch today for the dojo, I'd so appreciate it. I was going to come and help you, but Charlie has asked if I'll look after Ellie, but if it's really not possible…"

Rubbing her temple, Stacey rolled her eyes. Eleanor was a master manipulator, but she did it with such style, it was difficult to take offense. "It's okay, Eleanor. I'll make sure the dojo gets a poster, don't worry. By the way, we now have a bachelor number ten."

"Oh, lovely. I hope it is that handsome new hand over at River's Edge Ranch?"

"I was asked not to reveal his identity at this point, but I can tell you he's no ranch hand."

"Really? So who…?"

"Sorry, Eleanor, I have customers," she quickly said and ended the call, enjoying the rare moment of giving Eleanor a tiny taste of her own medicine. Even so, Eleanor had a way of getting any and all information she wanted. She'd have to try and stay out of the older woman's way for the next two and half weeks.

Frustrated, she grabbed the posters. She didn't want to go to the dojo. She didn't want to see Jason. It had been a crazy week. With Billie absent, she had to do everything herself. Normally she welcomed customers, but not if they were wasting her time.

Locking the door behind her, she jogged toward her car. She really, really hoped Blake was at the dojo today and not Jason. The very last thing she needed was to see him so soon after the weekend.

She started her car and quickly drove toward the dojo. She was tired and still rattled after her talk on Sunday with Christopher. Everything that had happened during her stay with her aunt had come back to her. What was clear at this point, though, was that she needed to talk to someone about her past to try and get some perspective.

On top of everything, she also missed Jason something fierce. He'd been haunting her dreams since she'd seen him with freaking Sandy Rivers on Sunday. Even though she hadn't caught even a glimpse of him since then, she could swear his scent was following her around. Those damn dopamine and norepinephrine levels were still sky-high, and she was afraid that situation wasn't going to change any time soon.

Wednesday, just before lunch, Jason walked toward his office to get his car keys. He was hungry and needed some air. As he passed Blake's office, Blake and Lindsay were just leaving.

Blake grabbed his arm. "Would you mind holding Laney for a bit?" he asked, and before Jason could respond, Blake handed him the small bundle wrapped in blankets. "I just want to walk with Lindsay to her car but it's so cold outside. I'll be back in a sec."

"I...don't..." he began.

Patting his arm, Lindsay smiled. "You're such a natural."

Like Lindsay had showed him on Monday, he put his one hand under the baby's head and cradled her in his arm.

"Look at you." Lindsay grinned. "As if you've been doing this for a long time." She glanced up at Blake. "Thanks for keeping an eye on Laney. Mom has her hands full with Ellie this morning but I knew Daddy wouldn't mind looking after his little girl while I have my hair cut. I should be back before her next feed. If she cries, change her nappy and walk with her, she likes that."

But Jason wasn't listening anymore, he was looking down at the tiny girl in his arms. Her eyes were closed. She was sleeping. Something shifted inside him. He held her even closer.

"Well, you seemed to know what you're doing," Blake joked as he returned.

"She's so small," Jason muttered as he stared at her button nose, her perfectly formed ears, and her tiny hands just peeping out from under the blanket.

"Blake?" a voice called from the doorway. Jason's heart leaped. It was Stacey.

"Hi, Stacey," Blake called out. "You coming to sign up for class again?"

Stacey shook her head as she took off her coat. "Eleanor asks if we may put up posters for the upcoming bachelors' auction on your windows?"

Blake laughed. "Seeing as one of the owners of the dojo is a bachelor, we can't really refuse, now, can we? Jason will help you. I'm on daddy duty." Tenderly, he took the baby from Blake.

"I don't need help," Stacey said quickly. "Just tell me where…"

"Jason will be happy to show you," Blake said, and with a wave he walked toward his office.

"Sorry about this," Stacey said, clearly uncomfortable to be alone with him.

"Sure," he said and walked in the direction of one of the big windows. "One here and one over there?" he asked, pointing toward the other window.

"Perfect, thanks."

As she bent to put the one poster down, he held out his hand. "Let me help you."

Nodding, she handed him the poster. Their fingers met fleetingly. Her breath hitched and blue eyes met his.

"Those darn chemical levels haven't subsided yet, have they?" he drawled.

Her face flaming, she turned her back on him and quickly put up the poster.

"I can do the last one on my own," she said, taking the poster from him.

He stayed where he was as she marched toward the other window. Minutes later, she was done and turned back. "Oh…I thought you'd left."

"Nope. Still standing here. Looking at you," he said.

Slowly, she approached him. "Don't say that." Her soft voice was enough to make his wayward hormones misbehave even more.

"I've missed you."

"Are you not with Sandy now?"

"Damn it to hell, Stace…" Taking her hand, he walked toward his office.

She tried to extract herself. "I…I have to go."

"Please?"

"Okay, you have two minutes," she said, chin in the air.

He locked his office door behind them and turned around quickly.

"What…what are you doing?"

He tucked a strand of hair behind her ear. "If I have only two minutes…" Bending his head, he let his lips trail down her cheek. "… I'm not wasting it trying to explain." His mouth hovered over hers, giving her time to move away if she wanted to, but with a groan, she grabbed his T-shirt with both hands.

"You make me crazy."

"Ditto," he got out before their mouths met in a fierce duel. He couldn't get enough of her and grabbing her very sexy butt in both his hands, he lifted her against him. Those long, gorgeous legs slipped around his body and he held on tightly.

As if a torrent had picked her up, Stacey was helpless to do anything else but cling to Jason. Angling his head, he deepened the kiss. Their tongues met in a happy dance.

Seeing him with little Laney in his arms, looking quite at ease, had nearly sent her racing back to her car again. *Babies…*

Jason's hand slipped down her side, his thumbs gazing her breasts, and every other thought disappeared. Pleasure tore through her, heating her blood, sending her heart into a frenzy. The only thought in this moment was that Jason wouldn't stop—must not stop—what he was doing.

"I have to see you, Stace." He moaned against her mouth as he put her gently down on a countertop. Keeping his eyes on her, he stepped in between her legs, his hands going for the buttons on her shirt.

While he was talking, she slid her hands underneath his T-shirt. His eyes darkening, he plucked it over his head before his fingers found the next button on her shirt.

Spreading her hands out over his chest, she exhaled slowly. Up close, his muscles were even more impressive.

"Stace, baby, you're killing me." Jason groaned. "Of course, you'd be wearing red lace. Damn. You're so, so beautiful."

He'd opened most of the buttons on her shirt, she saw as she looked down at herself. Heavy in anticipation for his touch, her breasts were straining against the lace, her nipples painfully hard. With a groan, he slipped a hand beneath her bra.

"Jason," she pleaded, not sure what for.

Slipping her breast from its constraint, he bent down, closing his mouth over one aching nipple. With a cry, she spun out of control. Grabbing hold of his head, she held on tightly as she tumbled down and down and down.

His own body throbbing with need, Jason watched in awe as Stacey crested. Inside him, something broke free. She opened her eyes, desire still lurking in the depths, her mouth swollen from his kisses.

"Beautiful," he whispered, cupping her face.

"Jason!" a voice called from outside. "The next class is about to begin."

Muttering, Stacey jumped from the cupboard. "I'm sorry..." she began, but he bent down and kissed her.

"Don't you dare say that. There's nothing to be sorry for. I'll see you tonight. I'll bring steaks."

"Jason, I don't think..."

"Then don't. Think, that is. We can dissect this whole thing to death, but bottom line is, I want you and after what has just happened, I know you want me too. Tonight. Seven o'clock. And oh, I think you should take a minute.

Your buttons need attention." His body burning with need, he traced the outline of one of her breasts with his fingertip.

Her eyes darkened and he simply had to kiss her again. Her mouth softened and opened underneath his onslaught.

Breathing hard, he forced himself to lift his head. "You'll be the death of me yet. See you tonight."

Her body still humming from Jason's touch, Stacey got into her car. Inhaling deeply, she dropped her forehead on the steering wheel. Oh, my goodness, what Jason could do to her with just a look… She forgot all about her resolve not to get involved with him.

With unsteady fingers, she took out her phone. The first message was to Jason, telling him she'd cook, he didn't have to bring steaks, and the second text was to the group chat she shared with Charlie, Lindsay, and Brooke, inviting them all to dinner.

With her freaking dopamine and norepinephrine levels not showing signs of settling down any time soon, she didn't dare spend an evening alone in Jason's company. With other people around, they'd have to talk. And with any luck, they'd probably discover they had nothing whatsoever in common.

Relaxing ever so slightly, she started her car. If she was going to have people over, she'd have to go the shops. He cupboards and fridge were bare. She hadn't had much appetite for a while. Those damn chemical levels…

CHAPTER 9

Stacey glanced at her watch before she turned around and smiled at her guests. So far she'd managed not to drop anything, but Jason would be arriving any minute now and then she wouldn't be able to guarantee anything. Oh, damn, those silly butterflies were back.

Lindsay and Blake had arrived in their own car so that they could leave, should Laney be a problem, and Charlie and Logan had driven into town with Brooke and Gavin.

"I'm so sorry your mom couldn't make it," Stacey said while opening a bottle of wine. "You do know you're more than welcome to bring the kids with you."

"We were going to," Charlie said, "but Eleanor insisted on looking after them. I was amazed, but she's been so busy organizing the bachelor auction, maybe she's just tired. Thank you for inviting us, though," she continued, her eyes twinkling. "I'm dying to hear whether all the rumors are true."

Before Stacey could answer her, the doorbell rang again. Her heart just about jumped out of her body.

"Expecting more company?" Brooke asked.

"Yes…uhm…Jason." Rattled, she bent down to open the oven door. The food was fine; she wasn't. She needed another minute. "Would someone mind getting the door? I need to…uhm…dinner…"

"I'll get it," Blake said, and left the room.

Her eyes dancing with mirth, Charlie approached Stacey. "Didn't you check the oven a few seconds ago?"

"Yeah, but…"

"Look who I found on your doorstep," Blake called out behind them. "With flowers, chocolates, and wine."

Bracing herself, Stacey turned toward the new arrival.

Blue eyes met hers briefly. "Didn't know what kind of flowers you like, so I got one of each," he said, shoving a gorgeous bunch of flowers in her hands. The chocolates and wine he put on the table before he turned around to greet the other guests.

Burying her face in the flowers, Stacey exhaled slowly. Jason was ticked off, that much she'd been able to see in the millisecond their eyes had met.

Well, that was too bad. She could invite other people to her house if she wanted to. Quickly, she put the flowers in a vase. "Thanks for the wine," she said as she picked up the bottle. Surprised, she saw the label. "A Shiraz…"

"Your favorite, if I remember correctly," he said as he walked back to where she was standing.

Flustered, she picked up the open bottle. "Wine?"

"I can help myself," he said, taking it from her.

Briefly, their fingers met. The fleeting connection left her breathless and shaken. Oh, my goodness, it was going to be a long night. Those freaking hormones—not ever a room full of other people could prevent her from wanting to jump Jason's bones.

Plastering a smile on her face, she motioned toward the table. "If everyone has wine, let's sit down."

Jason deliberately took a chair opposite Stacey. There was no way he'd be able to keep his hands to himself if he sat next to her. This way, he could watch her, though.

She was rattled. He'd been so fed up with her when he'd arrived to see she'd invited other people, he hadn't immediately noticed her nervousness. But facing her, he was aware of everything about her. Even though she was doing her best to look calm and collected, the frantic beating of the pulse against her neck was a clear giveaway.

And damn it, she looked gorgeous. Her red hair was hanging loose tonight, cascading in curls down her back. The white cross-over top of sheer material she was wearing with a pair of tight-fitting jeans had his fingers itching. If he wasn't mistaken, the bands of the top were tied together in just one knot, which meant…

Within seconds all the blood had moved to way below his middle. Uncomfortable, he moved in his chair.

"…who is bachelor number ten?" Charlie's voice finally penetrated his lustful thoughts.

Smiling, Stacey shook her head. "I know who it is, but he wants to keep it a secret until the night of the auction. Trust me, I'm dying to tell you, but I've made a promise."

"So, it's not the young man you had coffee with on Sunday morning?" Brooke asked.

Rolling her eyes, Stacey groaned out load. "Seriously, this town. The young man I had coffee with is Christopher, a cousin from South Africa. He was just passing through." She briefly met Jason's gaze before she continued.

"But that's wonderful," Charlie said. "Did you know he was coming to visit?"

"No, we've lost touch," she quickly replied before she picked up a spoon. "More meat anyone?"

"Yes, please," he said, lifting his plate. It was obvious she wanted to change the subject. The small, grateful smile in his direction made him feel ten feet tall. The woman was driving him crazy. The one minute he wanted to throttle her, the next she smiled at him and he forgot his irritation.

She had him nicely tied up in knots, not a feeling he was comfortable with.

After dinner, Jason got up quickly. "Why don't you ladies go and sit in the living room, we'll wash the dishes."

"Don't be silly," Stacey protested as she got up. "I'll do it later—"

But both Charlie and Lindsay jumped up and grabbing her hand, they dragged her toward the living room.

"Never ever say no if a man offers to do the cleaning up." Brooke smiled. "One of the first things my mom has taught me."

"I just feel so bad. Everyone has worked today—"

"Come on, put up your feet. That was a fantastic meal," Charlie said. "You deserve to relax."

They all found a place to sit before they eagerly leaned forward. "So," Charlie whispered. "You've also invited Jason? Does that mean you're dating?"

"No!" Stacey quickly cried out softly. "He... I... "

"She's stuttering," Charlie said.

"She is indeed," Lindsay teased. "Our Stacey here is always in control. She never stutters, she always knows what she wants to say."

"The man can't keep his eyes off of you." Brooke smiled. "The electrical currents between the two of you are powerful."

"I'm not in the market for a relationship," Stacey said, repeating the words she'd always hid behind.

"Why ever not?" Charlie asked. "When Lindsay and I moved here, meeting someone, getting married, was the last thing on our minds. I was under the impression I couldn't have kids, remember? And then Logan walked into my office..."

"And after my horrible experience with my last relationship, I just wanted to get on with my life. Marriage and babies were definitely not in the picture. But then..." Grinning, she motioned to where the men were cleaning the kitchen. "Blake insisted on protecting me."

"And I didn't think I'd get another chance at love," Brooke said. "But now I can't picture my life without Gavin. And he's so good with Connor. And bonus—he cooks!"

Stacey shook her head. "I'm so happy for all of you, I really am, but please believe me when I tell you I'm very happily single. Getting married, having babies—those things are not a part of my future."

Charlie patted Stacey's shoulder. "All I can tell you is that you literally light up every time you see Jason. You guys have so much in common; it would be such a pity not to pursue a relationship."

"Have you noticed they even finish one another's sentences?" Lindsay smiled. "He seems to know what she's going to say even before she says it. And you are clearly in tune with him, Stacey."

Uncomfortable, Stacey rubbed her face. Lindsay was right. The conversation around the table had moved from politics to saving the environment to movies and music. Instead of pointing out how different they were, the banter around the table had actually confirmed how much she and Jason agreed on basic principles.

Brooke leaned forward. "We're interfering, I know, and help me, I sound just like my mother, but you and Jason are so obviously—"

"There is no Jason and me," Stacey said again.

Brooke just smiled but thankfully she changed the topic. "So, will you see your cousin again?" Brooke asked.

"Maybe." Briefly she told them about Christopher's trip and that he might stop by on his way to Bozeman.

"You must miss you family back home," Charlie said.

"I haven't had any contact with them since I've moved here. It's...uhm...complicated."

"Families usually are." Charlie smiled. "If ever you want to talk about it, we're here for you, okay?"

With a sigh, Stacey glanced at the three women. She knew them, knew they wouldn't gossip about anything she told them. "I've never been comfortable talking about my past. It's not as if I'd been abused or anything, but the feeling of not having any control isn't something I seem to be able to forget. I went to live with my Aunt Penelope when I was twelve."

In a shortened version, she quickly told them about the time she'd spent with her aunt's family and how helpless she'd felt.

"Oh, my goodness!" Charlie said softly, and hugged Stacey. "You were twelve. No wonder you're wary of babies."

Lindsay's eyes were swimming in tears. "Oh, Stacey, I'm so sorry you had to go through that. Not having control over your own life because someone else had taken it away, I understand. But look at you, you've done so well for yourself."

"I've worked hard to get here, to be able to do what I want when I want," Stacey said. "And when you get married and have kids, you give it all up, don't you? I don't ever want to do that again."

Lindsay frowned. "All three of us are still doing what we love even though we're married and have kids. I think I understand your fear, but don't let that stop you from opening your heart to love—that would be such a pity."

"I know you've just given us the short version of what has happened to you, but maybe you should see a professional, you know? What you've been through is obviously still haunting you," Brooke said.

Fortunately, the men chose that moment to join them, saving Stacey from having to answer. Since she'd spoken to Christopher on Sunday and had told Jason something about the time she'd been living with her aunt, she'd been unable to shove away the unpleasant thoughts from her past the way she'd been doing over the last eight years.

All those feelings she'd experienced at the time had returned, making her restless and unsure of herself. Maybe she should consider talking to someone about her past at some point.

As Stacey walked her guests outside to see them off, Jason stayed behind in the kitchen, putting away the clean dishes. She wasn't going to get rid of him that easily.

As the last car drove away, Stacey returned, fidgeting with that damn knot on her top. "I...thanks for everything you've brought. The wine, the chocolates, the flowers."

Slowly, he walked toward her. "So you thought inviting your friends here tonight as well would keep me from wanting to touch you?"

She crossed her arms. "I'm sorry if you're angry, but it's for the best. Spending more time with you is not the solution. Those stupid dopamine and norepinephrine levels are still sky-high. Look what happened this afternoon! The kissing and the touching are just making it worse."

Amused, he leaned against the kitchen counter. "Really?"

"Yes, I was quite content with my life, happy to be single. But then I met you and everything changed. For the past year, I've managed to avoid you, though, and I was fine, but since I've been helping Eleanor with the bachelor auction, you're everywhere—in the camera with your damn cocky grin, your unbuttoned shirt..." Groaning, she rubbed her temple. "See? I tell you things I'll never tell anyone else!"

Jason had a difficult time not grinning. "And you think the solution would be to keep out of each other's way?"

"Yes."

"For how long?"

"I don't know!"

"You're the one who's telling me this is just biology. Surely there should be time limit if it's only biology? Until the auction?"

"It's been a year since I saw you first but okay... yes.

I'm sure if we put our minds to it, we can get this craziness out of our systems by next weekend."

"Okay." Moving closer, he slipped a hand under her hair. "Seeing that those levels are skyrocketing at the moment anyway…" Bending down, he kissed her.

Her soft sigh exploded inside his mouth, sending tremors echoing through his body. Silky arms slipped around his neck, soft curves fitted perfectly against his chest. He kept his hands where they were, concentrating on the kiss, licking and nibbling and savoring the softness of her mouth.

Only when she was shuddering in his arms and he was ready to explode, did he lift his head and step back.

He had to gulp in some fresh air before he could talk. "So according to your calculations, we'll stop wanting to tear each other's clothes off by next weekend, when it's the bachelor auction?"

"Yes, if you stay away from me," she said, her breathing ragged like his. "You should take out some of the available single ladies in town."

"You're serious?" he got out. "I'm aching for you and you want me to see other women?"

"Neither of us is interested in anything long-term, that we've already established, and I'm not in the market for casual sex and you…well, you're obviously in need of sex. Date some of the other single women in town. By next weekend you'll have forgotten all about this craziness between us."

"Damn it, it's not about having sex!"

"Of course it is. You were very clear about not wanting to get married."

"I…we…" Cussing below his breath, he stomped out. He'd probably be a dead man by next weekend. A cold shower. That was what he needed right now. More than one, if the state of his body was anything to go by. But she was right, he wasn't interested in anything long-term and whether Stacey wanted to know it or not, she'd make some lucky guy very happy.

Damn it, he didn't want to think about Stacey with anyone else. Inhaling deeply, he got into his car.

He liked women, but since he'd laid eyes on Stacey, he hadn't even noticed any other woman. And now she was the one telling him to see other women? Have sex with them?

As he drove away, he turned to look back at Stacey's house. She was standing on the porch, staring after him. Grinding his teeth, he stepped on the gas. Okay, he'd date other people. There were a number of beautiful, willing single ladies around town. Maybe it was time to shift his focus from the redhead and meet more of the single ladies of Alisson, Montana. Have sex with them, even.

Maybe one of them would be able to assuage this ache inside his belly.

He'd never even considered staying with just one woman.

But as he drove home, the only woman he could think of was Stacey.

ELSA WINCKLER

CHAPTER 10

By the next Wednesday, the whole town was abuzz with auction fever. Billie was feeling better and was back at work, but she'd been so preoccupied with all things bachelor auction, to Stacey's frustration, her assistant didn't get anything else done.

Stacey had finished the menu of the bachelors over the weekend and had given it to Billie to print. However, Billie had apparently spent so much time browsing through all the info of the bachelors and sharing it with everyone she knew, she hadn't gotten around to actually finishing printing it.

"It's called marketing," Billie defended herself. "I'm just sharing what I know about the bachelors so that people will know who exactly they're bidding on."

It was late afternoon, nearly closing time, but again the bell above the door chimed, announcing more customers. Leaving Billie to finish the printing, Stacey moved to the front of the shop. Guy Richard had walked in.

"Mr. Richard!" Stacey smiled. She hadn't seen the older man since he'd announced his willingness to be bachelor number ten. "Are you ready for Saturday night?" she asked softly.

"Ready as I'll ever be," he said, looking around to make sure they were alone. "Nobody else knows about this, right?"

Before Stacey could answer, the bell chimed again and in strolled Eleanor. Her usually wide smile was in place until she saw Guy Richard. She was about to turn around when the door opened again and Brooke and Lindsay, with her baby in her arms, entered as well.

"Mr. Richard!" Brooke greeted the older man. "I haven't seen you since our wedding. How have you been?"

"Hallo, Brooke, Lindsay.," He nodded before he looked at their mother. "Eleanor. You've been ignoring my calls."

"I did no such thing," Eleanor said quickly. "I've been busy. You've probably heard about the bachelor auction?"

"Indeed, I have," he said, a small smile hovering around his lips. "So will you be bidding on any of the bachelors?" he asked her.

Eleanor fidgeted. "Of course not! I'm organizing the whole thing; I can't bid."

"Nonsense, of course, you can," Stacey said. "Everyone else on the committee has already indicated they'll be bidding as well. Remember, it's all for a good cause."

"Well, we'll see," Eleanor said. "I'm sure I'll be far too busy to behind the scenes. I'm just stopping by to find out whether you need anything from me, Stacey?"

"No, thanks, Eleanor. We have it all under control."

"So you'll bring the menus on Saturday evening and help me to distribute them?"

"Yes, Billie and I will be there."

"And bachelor number ten? When do we get to see him?" Eleanor asked.

"He'll be there!" Stacey nodded, forcing herself not to glance in Guy Richard's direction.

Just then the door to her shop opened again and in strolled Sandy Rivers. Stacey swallowed a groan. She knew exactly why Sandy was here. Stacey had heard the latest talk: Jason had taken Sandy to dinner on Saturday night and Sandy probably wanted to make sure everyone knew about it. Especially Stacey.

"Good morning, everyone," Sandy smiled. "Oooh, I can't wait for Saturday night's auction. I know exactly who I'll be bidding on. I hope everyone knows by now I'm going to bid on and win a date with a certain dojo owner."

Eleanor smiled. "Well, I have to warn you, the competition is fierce. Joni Moore had breakfast with him this morning and she's also set on winning his bid."

"Joni Moore?" snorted Sandy. "She doesn't stand a chance."

"And then there's Cindi Harris, the librarian. Apparently, they'd gone skating together," Charlie added.

"Well, we'll just have to see, won't we?" Sandy said crossly before she quickly left.

Stacey kept a smile on her face even though her heart was breaking into small pieces with the mention of each of the town beauties.

Jason had apparently taken her advice to heart and had begun to woo the single ladies of the town. While she couldn't eat or sleep for missing him, he has been seen around town with a new woman on his arm every day.

He was doing what she'd suggested, though—so why did she feel like crying?

"Well, things are heating up for Saturday night, that's for sure." Eleanor laughed. "The ladies of the bridge club are also fired up and will give Sandy a run for her money, I'm afraid. Dottie Hanson is just as determined to win a date with Jason."

Brooke inhaled sharply. "Dottie Hanson? Isn't she a hundred?"

"A hundred and one, actually," Eleanor grinned. "But she's got money and she's very happy to give it up for…charity."

Just then Stacey's phone rang. It was Christopher. For

a millisecond she wavered. Did she want to talk to him again? But as soon as the thought entered her mind, she dismissed it. Of course she did. He was a sweet kid; she'd always liked him. Quickly, Stacey waved to Billie, indicating she should come and see to the customers while Stacey rushed to her office.

"Christopher, hi. Are you back from your hike?"

"Yes, we're on our way to Bozeman to catch a flight later tonight, but I was hoping I could pop into your shop quickly to say a final goodbye?"

"Of course. It's a bit chaotic at the moment. The town has a bachelor auction on Saturday night."

"Bachelor auction!" Christopher laughed. "I've never heard of that before. But I won't keep you long," he said. "I'll be there in about five minutes."

When Stacey returned to the front of the shop after her call, Guy had left.

"I hope you haven't chased Mr. Richard away?" Stacey joked.

"Mother has been strangely rude," Brooke said, her eyes twinkling. "He was such a fabulous date to you on our wedding, Mom I don't know why you won't see him again."

"I'm too old for such silliness," Eleanor said.

Brooke shook her head. "No, you're not. Maybe you and Stacey here should both talk to a professional about your fear of relationships." Brooke's eyes clouded. "I've told Mom about your experience living with your aunt."

Eleanor grabbed hold of Stacey's hands. "I'm so sorry you had to go through that, sweetie. I'll support you in any way that I can. Talking to someone about the traumas in our lives is always a good idea. I'll text you the name of someone I know in Butte. She's an old friend and she's very good at what she does."

"While you're at it, why don't you make an appointment for yourself as well? Running away from Guy Richard is ridiculous, and you know it." Brooke asked.

"Yes, Eleanor," Lindsay said, "you deserve to be happy. Talk to someone if you have a problem. The man is obviously crazy about you."

Eleanor patted her daughter's hand. "I've been married, my dear. I'm way too old and cranky to change my ways for anyone. Anyway, he or I can die at any moment. What fun would that be for the one left behind? Come on, we've kept Stacey busy long enough."

Over Eleanor's head, Brooke winked at her as the women left Stacey's shop.

Stacey sighed. For such a long time, she'd just tried to forget about her past but now she'd seen her cousin and had told a number of people a little bit about it. She was already feeling less burdened.

Maybe talking to a professional would help.

As Jason opened his car door for Cora Mendelsohn to get out, he glanced up. Stacey was just exiting her shop as a young man walked toward her. Her cousin, if he wasn't mistaken. Christopher was probably back from his hiking trip.

"I was wondering where you're taking me?" Cora smiled as she got out.

As Cora took his arm, his gaze was still on Stacey across the street. She looked up and for a moment, their eyes met. His heart kicked against his ribs. Just a glimpse of her was enough to leave him aching for her. Damn it.

Trying to focus on Cora, he opened the door of the coffee shop. Cora had been attending his dojo classes over the last month. She was pretty and nice and maybe she'd be able to make him forget about Stacey, even it was only for an hour. That was what he'd thought when he'd invited her for coffee after class.

None of the other women he'd taken on a date this week had interested him even a little bit. The idea of having sex with anyone else than Stacey simply hadn't even entered his mind. They were all pretty and cute and obviously keen to go on a second date but they were not the ones he wanted to be with. They weren't Stacey.

As he and Cora sat down, he glanced over to Stacey's shop again. She and her cousin entered her shop and the door closed behind them. Would she be okay? Why was he here again? Was there still something he wanted to tell her, something that might upset her?

Not your problem, remember? The waitress, a high school student, approached, her eyes twinkling. She'd been serving him and all the other dates he'd brought around for coffee this week.

"So what are we having today?" she asked, her eyes dancing with mirth.

"A cappuccino for me, thanks, Lizzie," Cora said.

"And for you? Black coffee?"

"Thanks, yes." He nodded. As she walked away, he tried to focus on Cora. "So Cora, tell me about your job? You work at the pharmacy?"

"Yes, I do. I started working there right out of school…"

As Cora's voice droned on, he looked at her, trying to focus on what she was saying. But instead of her short blond hair, all he could see was Stacey's red curls hanging over a satiny shoulder, teasing him.

His heart sighed. It was time to accept the inevitable. While he had Stacey Lawrence on his brain and in his blood, no other woman would do.

"I hope you don't mind," Christopher said as he took out his phone, "but when I told the twins I've run into you, they wanted to speak to you as well. Would you mind if we phone them? It's about midnight in South Africa now, but they're preparing for the end-of-year school exams and would really like to talk to you. Of course, if you don't feel like it, we can try and do it at a later stage that would suit you."

Stunned, Stacey swallowed. It was one thing to talk to Christopher, but talking to the twins? "Wow, they'll be finishing school next year, it's hard to imagine. I don't know but…okay, yes, let's do it. I'd love to talk to them."

Minutes later, the twins' faces were on the small screen of Christopher's phone. The last time she'd seen them, they'd been nine. That was the picture she'd been carrying around with her all this time.

"Look at you," she smiled, feeling tearful. "You're all grown up. Penny, you're gorgeous and Kev, you've grown into such a handsome young man."

They started talking simultaneously and she really tried to keep up but she couldn't understand a word they were saying.

Laughing, Christopher intervened. "One at a time, guys."

Penny took the phone. "Stacey, it's so good to see you again. You know, I still remember all the stories you read to us. A bunny saying goodnight…" Penny looked at her brother. "Do you remember?"

"*Goodnight Moon*?" Stacey asked in delight.

"Yes," Kevin said. "And there was one about a caterpillar…"

Stacey smiled. "*The Very Hungry Caterpillar*? I read you all the stories my mom used to read to me."

"Yes, and do you remember…?" Penny started naming all the stories she could, with Kevin and sometimes even Christopher chipping in.

"What about you?" Penny asked eventually. "Tell us about yourself. What do you do? When did you move to Alisson?"

Happy, Stacey told them about her shop and what she did. "Basically, it's a I'll-fix-your-computer-problems shop."

"I'm impressed." Penny smiled. "Christopher mentioned a Jason you had dinner with—is he the boyfriend?"

"No!" Stacey denied the notion quickly. "No boyfriend. Marriage isn't for me."

"That would be such a pity." Penny smiled. "You should marry and have lots of babies. You'll be such a great mom." Sobering, she sniffled. "We were too small to understand what was going on with our mom, but I do remember feeling safe when I was with you."

"Me too," Kevin piped in. "We've spoken to Dad and if it's okay with you, we'd like to come and visit you by the end of next year when we finish school?"

"We can feed ourselves nowadays!" Penny chuckled. "And you've potty trained us, remember?"

Her head reeling, Stacey felt herself nodding. The reason she'd crossed an ocean, moved to a small town situated on another continent, was so that she'd never be reminded again of the time when she didn't have any control over her life.

She'd held on so tightly to the belief she was finally at a place where she dictated her own future, where she could plan her life according to her wishes, she'd never for a minute thought about the impact her leaving had on the three kids who had been in her care. In contrast with her own memories, they remembered her fondly. They actually wanted to spend time with her.

"Okay, guys, I'll see you in a few days' time," Christopher was saying as he ended the call. He touched her shoulder. "I have to go, but thanks for talking to them, for making time to see me one more time. I know it can't be easy for you." He checked his watch. "The others are waiting at the bar. We have a flight to catch to Amsterdam and from there to Cape Town."

She followed him outside. "It was so good to see you, Christopher, and it was lovely to talk to the twins. Thank you. I'm sorry I haven't kept in touch…"

"We don't blame you, okay? But it would be nice if we can talk to you now and again? And I'll like to come with the twins when they visit you."

"I'd like that. You have my number. Any time."

Grinning, he bent down and gave her a fierce hug. "Bye, cuz. I want to hear all about the Bachelor Auction when I call you!" With a wave, he sprinted across the street.

Feeling like crying, she quickly turned and walked back into her shop. She'd been nursing the hurt and anger she'd felt when she thought about the time she'd lived with her aunt. She still got nightmares of her aunt screaming at her or berating her for something. Because of that, she'd cut her cousins out of her life as well, something she was very sorry for now. It hadn't been all bad. She'd really enjoyed the kids. It had been the constant pressure from her aunt she'd fled from.

Maybe I should talk to someone...

As the thought popped into her head again, she looked across the street. Jason and his date were on their way to his car. Were they on their way to his house or hers?

Argh, she didn't want to know. She waited for his car to leave before she grabbed her coat and laptop. She had a new book and left-over soup from last night. A peaceful night, just like she preferred.

Maybe she should just stop at the grocery store. Sometimes they had fresh rolls this time of day.

Somehow the idea of at home, all alone, had lost its shine.

ELSA WINCKLER

CHAPTER 11

There were still a few people in the grocery store as Jason entered. He'd just dropped off Cora. He probably should've taken her to dinner. At least then he'd have had a meal out of the evening.

Problem was, he didn't want to be with Cora or Sandy or whatever other woman he'd tried to date over the last few days. There was only one woman's presence he craved but she refused to accept they should spend time together. His tummy growled. A man had to eat, so he was going to pick up something ready to microwave at home.

The cry of a baby from the direction of the cashiers caught his attention. Sophie McNeally, the high school football coach's wife, was trying to pay for her groceries but her ten-month-old baby was protesting loudly. Her two-year-old twins were making things even harder by chasing each other around the haggard-looking cashier.

As he stepped forward to see if he could help the poor woman, the arms of someone standing behind Sophie, reached out and took the baby from her. As the person moved forward, he recognized her. It was Stacey.

Stunned, he stared as the redhead put her own basket to the side and continued to talk to the baby. While Sophie was paying for her groceries and rounding up the twins, Stacey walked with the baby over to the toys, where she continued a running conversation with baby. He was too far away to hear what she was saying, but the baby had stopped crying and was looking up at Stacey in wonder.

Eventually, the flustered mother was finished paying for her shopping and Stacey handed the baby back to Sophie.

The line moved forward but instead of picking up her basket and getting back into the queue to pay for the groceries, Stacey ignored it and headed out of the store.

With long strides, he walked to where she'd left the basket and picked it up. He knew what had just happened: Stacey had held the baby and was upset.

Looking down at the contents of her basket, he shook his head. What a pitiful dinner. Surely, he could do better than a loaf of bread and a block of cheese?

Stacey closed the door behind her, took off her coat, and dropped her car keys on the kitchen counter. Her hands still had the slightly powdery smell of the baby on them. She'd actually held a baby and she hadn't had a meltdown.

The moment she'd heard about her grandmother's inheritance all those years ago, she'd stopped babysitting, but for years afterward, she'd still hear babies cry at random times. For the past eight years, she'd steered clear of babies and talk of babies, convinced she'd freak out completely if anyone were to put one in her arms. But tonight, poor Sophie had been so obviously in need of a little help, Stacey had taken the baby from her without really thinking about what she was doing.

Babies reacted well to soothing voices, she'd learned when she was struggling to keep the twins from crying and bothering their mother, and that was what she'd reverted to tonight. There were so many sounds in a place like a grocery store, no wonder the poor thing was crying—it could all be a bit overwhelming.

The bell at the front door chimed. Frowning, she walked toward it. Maybe Christopher wanted to ask her something again or… She opened the door. Her heart sighed.

"Jason," she got out. "Don't you have a date? You have been busy, I hear—"

"Have you eaten?" he interrupted her as he stepped inside.

"No, but…"

He lifted the bags he was holding in his hands. "You left your groceries in the store."

"Oh…yes, I…"

"Helped poor Sophie."

"So you saw me with the baby?"

"I did. You're a natural, did you know that? Are you okay? I know you're not big on babies."

Oh, and her stupid heart melted a little bit. He was worried about her. "I'm okay. But you really didn't have to…"

Closing the door behind him, he walked toward the kitchen with the two bags of groceries. "I've done what you've suggested and dated other women. What I can tell you now—and this is something I've told you already—is I don't want to be with any other woman. I certainly don't want to have sex with any of them. So can we sit down and have dinner and not talk about other women? The only woman I want to be with," he said as he put the bags down, removed his jacket, and turned back to her, "is you."

"Jason…"

Afterward, she was never sure who moved first, but the next moment she was in his arms, his lips ravaging hers. The little voice piped up trying to stop her, but the need to be with him, was too raw, too insistent. She couldn't get enough of him. With every breath she took, she inhaled his musky maleness until she was steeped in his scent. Her eager fingers were tearing at his clothes, desperate to touch him without any obstacles in the way.

With an oath, he plucked his shirt over his head before his mouth descended on hers again—hot, hungry, demanding. He toyed with her mouth; she let him. Her hands glided happily over his naked, hot flesh.

This was madness, but she hoped it would never end. She couldn't think of any other place she'd rather be than here, kissing Jason. Her hands slid around him, over his body, exploring the hard ridge of muscle up his back.

Nearly frantic, he tugged down the neckline of her top, latched his mouth on her throat. Those busy hands traveled down her sides, found their way underneath her top while his mouth moved desperately over her breast before it finally closed around an aching nipple.

Cradling his head, she gave herself up to his ministrations, reveling in the strong arms holding her tightly, his ragged breathing..

With a soft cuss, he swept her up and hugging her closer to him, he staggered down the corridor. "Which way?"

"First room," she got out. It was difficult to talk; her attention was wandering. Firm muscles, begging to be explored, were right in front of her eyes. In awe, she spread her fingers over his chest in an effort to touch as much of his skin as possible. She breathed him in, felt his heart tripping under her fingers just before he slid her down his body. They were next to her bed.

Outside, the sun was setting, people were going about their evening routines. She was only vaguely aware of the outside sounds. Her room was full of moving shadows, but her eyes were only fixed on the big man.

Excitement was building up, prickling along her skin, as those big hands lifted her top over her head and dropped it. With his eyes on her, he shuddered, not afraid to show how their intimacy affected him. She unclasped her bra, watched his eyes darken as those big hands cupped her breasts.

She'd dreamt about being with him but nothing her imagination had conjured up came close to the very real heat between them, or could have prepared her for the way one look of those blue eyes managed to dissolve the little control she had left.

With infinite care, he picked her up and laid her on the bed. While his eyes raked over her body, he quickly tried to get out of his jeans. But his boots were in the way, and cussing and struggling, he sat down to get rid of them.

Laughing, she reared up, slid her arms around his body, and pressed her aching breasts against his hot flesh.

"The damn boots," he muttered before he finally kicked his jeans away. Quickly turning around, he bent over her, crushing her lips with his.

Breaths mingled; tongues met in a joyous dance. Her hands slid over powerful muscles. He was naked and she was free to touch him.

Why had she fought so hard against this?

In reverence, Jason lifted his head, stroked his hands over satiny skin, toned lines, and luscious curves. "You are...so, so beautiful," he murmured as his mouth followed the soft line of her shoulder. The smell of camellias seeped through his pores, rushed through his blood, sending his heartbeat into overdrive.

Impatient to see more of her, he fumbled with the button on her jeans. Gasping, she helped him, lifting her hips so he could peel them from her.

All she was left wearing was a small red lace triangle. "Damn, Stace, you're killing me," he whispered as he bent down to worship her breasts. Her skin was already damp from the heat. The air around them was thick, making breathing more and more difficult.

The fire she'd unleashed was burning hot and bright,

heating his body to an unbearable point. Impatiently, he tried to pull the piece of red lace down her legs, but he didn't want to struggle anymore, he wanted her naked. Now. With a tug of his hands, he ripped it from her body, flinging it sideways before his mouth found hers again, swallowing her groan.

Their legs tangled, his free hand raked over her in a merciless assault, before he bent down and found her breast. He couldn't stop the groan of pleasure from deep within him. As she moved restlessly beneath him, he licked and nibbled and with her heartbeat hammering against his mouth, he lost himself in her taste, in the texture of her skin, in her.

He wanted her as much as she wanted him. She could feel the urgency racing through him, heard it in his quickening breath—a heady feeling. Her hips arched up to him, wordlessly telling him she needed him desperately.

Those clever fingers weren't done with her yet. Slipping farther down her body, he found her heat. She cried out as stars exploded behind her eyes. Stunned by the climax, she lay shuddering beneath him as he lifted his head to look at her.

"Beautiful. You are so beautiful," he murmured, his eyes dark, his face flushed. Before she could catch her next breath, he was kissing her again.

As his mouth plundered hers, her hands were roaming freely over his body, enjoying the feel of him. Control was gone. Giddily, she rolled with him, amazed at the intensity of her own need.

Only after she'd crested two more times did he hoist himself above her.

"Look at me," he demanded.

Helpless to do anything else, she held his gaze while he plunged forward, becoming one with her.

And in that moment, she understood the madness. A

soft sigh slipped out. Her eyes closed.

Oh, my goodness, she'd gone and fallen in love with Jason. That was why her stupid dopamine and norepinephrine levels wouldn't settle down. After all this time, she still couldn't be in the same room as him without wanting to hyperventilate.

There was biology and then there was love—two completely different things, she finally understood.

Despite her resolve never to marry, never to have kids, her heart had ignored all the messages from her brain and she'd fallen in love with this man anyway. He had her heart in his hands—not something that would ever change or "settle" or disappear.

Tears clogged up her throat as she welcomed him home, pulling him close to her.

Even if—and it was a big if—she'd somehow get over her fear of babies, of commitment and marriage, Jason been very clear about not ever wanting anything more permanent. So tonight was all they'd ever have; she shouldn't forget that. She was going to absorb every detail so that she could remember this forever.

For a moment they stayed like that, rasping breaths, trying to calm down, but desire was building once again, more intense, more passionate than before, and lifting his head, Jason began to move.

And as if they'd been doing this for a long time, she quickly found his rhythm. With her gaze locked with his, this time they raced up that steep hill together.

When Jason next opened his eyes, he was alone in the bed. Quickly, he got up, slipped on his jeans, and went looking for Stacey.

She was in the kitchen, making sandwiches, if he wasn't mistaken—in his shirt, with just one button done up. Desire slammed him in the gut and, stunned at the intensity of it, he tried to inhale. But it was difficult. His head was swimming, the embers catching fire again.

Humming, she swayed from side to side as she worked. Those gorgeous red tresses fell messily over her shoulders. He imagined it, the long, red locks skimming over pert breasts.

She looked up. His heart skipped a beat. He was a goner; had been since the moment he'd laid eyes on her.

"You're wearing my shirt," he said as he slowly approached her.

"You've ruined my panties," she said, licking the knife. The movement shot straight down to his groin. He simply had to be with her again.

With a soft oath, he reached her in another stride. This time the bedroom was too far away. With his gaze on hers, he lifted her onto the kitchen counter and stepped between her legs.

"I've made sandwiches."

"Later."

"Okay."

Unbuttoning the shirt, he pushed her back, and in one movement, swiped his hand down her body from her breast to her heat. Her eyes darkened and with a soft sigh, her head fell backward, giving him access to all of her softness.

With his blood roaring through his veins, he dropped his jeans and pushed into her. Home. This was home. Gathering her close to his heart, he buried his face in her hair. Her legs slipped around him, bringing him even closer to her and he began to move.

Her face was flushed with fresh fever, her body urging him on to move faster. With his heart pounding at an alarming rate, he increased the tempo and still she kept up with him, still she gave more.

When she finally shuddered against him, he was there with her, her name a desperate cry on his lips.

CHAPTER 12

The next time Stacey woke up, she dressed as quickly as her shaking hands allowed her to. The ripped pair of panties she put under a pillow and slipped on a clean pair. Jason was lying on his stomach on her bed, the sheet carelessly covering only a part of his buttocks.

Instantly, her mouth watered again and with a soft groan, she slipped from the room. What she wanted to do, what every fiber of her being was urging her to do, was to get right back into bed with him again.

It was just after midnight. Outside it was quiet; there was no movement. She put on the kettle before she walked toward the windows. Most of the houses in the street were dark. People were probably sleeping.

A sound behind her made her head turn. And there he was. Big, gorgeous, and so sexy, she throbbed with instant need. He was dressed. Inhaling deeply, she plastered a smile on her face.

"We never did get round to that sandwich," she said.

"Food was the last thing on my mind. Stacey—"

Lifting her hand, she stopped him from saying anything more. "Please, no explanations necessary. Neither one of us is looking for anything more, yada-yada, we don't have to re-hash the whole thing again."

Frowning, he walked right up to her. "I wasn't going to explain anything, except to say, I'll see you tomorrow night. This isn't over, not by a long shot."

"Sorry, I'm busy for the rest of the week, and you have an auction to prepare for."

His eyes narrowed. "You don't want to see me after what just happened between us?"

Slipping under his arm, she walked toward the front door. "We've had sex, Jason. Great sex, I'll give you that, but we both know this isn't going anywhere."

"Sex. Look me in the eye and tell me it was only sex for you."

She couldn't face him, though. "Just go. It's late and...the neighbors will talk." She couldn't give a damn what the neighbors would say, but he didn't have to know that.

He was quiet for a long time. "I didn't know you were a coward, Stacey. Guess I was wrong."

The next moment her front door opened and closed with a bang. She waited. Maggie spluttered a few times before she started. Jason drove away. Only then did Stacey let the first tears fall down her cheeks while a hysterical giggle also threatened to slip out.

She'd gone and fallen for a guy with a truck called Maggie.

Friday morning, Jason arrived early at the dojo. He hadn't slept the last two nights. Instead, he'd been pacing the corridor of his house 'til the early hours, thinking about Stacey, missing her.

The damn woman had him all tied up in knots and she called what happened between them sex? He'd had sex before. With a number of women. He wasn't proud of his past, but he'd been with enough women to know what had happened between him and Stacey last night hadn't been merely sex.

She'd been with him every single step of the way. Gorgeous, beautiful, and so sexy he ached just thinking about her lithe body pressing against him, the soft sounds she made every time she'd crested.

He'd been transported to another universe while being with her. What was more—he knew she'd experienced the same thing. She'd been hurt in the past, he got that, but surely she should know he'd never hurt her.

"Everything okay?" Blake's amused voice asked from behind him. "You look like a man with a woman on the mind. I'm just not sure which one? Rumor has it you've been up to your old tricks, keeping the single ladies of Alisson happy."

Jason glared at Blake. "I've...dated but only because she..." Muttering a curse, he pressed his lips together.

"She? Aaah. So, there *is* someone who has you all twisted up inside? All I can tell you is to do something about it. You'll remember how stupid I've been. Because I couldn't believe I was good enough for Lindsay I nearly lost her. I still shudder when I think of how very nearly I let her slip through my fingers. A life without her is not one I care to think about."

"This is not the same," Jason growled. "You've fallen in love with Lindsay but I..." A band tightened around his chest, making breathing difficult. "With us, it's different...just biology, she'd said so herself. Some or other chemical levels...oh, I remember, dopamine and norepinephrine levels are high at the moment, but it'll settle. I was told just to be patient."

Blake burst out laughing. "Oh, man, this is so pathetic. You're head over heels in love with the woman. You have been for the past year. Everyone can see it, except you. It's much more than biology and you know it." Shaking his head, Blake turned away.

The first class was about to begin but Jason was only vaguely aware of the students entering the dojo.

Surely, he wasn't in love with Stacey—what a ridiculous idea. He wasn't the marrying kind. He enjoyed seeing a number of women...

His blood rushed through his veins. The loud roaring in his head made him catch his breath. No, he didn't. Not anymore. He should be honest with himself, at least. No other woman had interested him since... well, since the first day he'd noticed Stacey in this very class. In that moment, everything had changed.

His mind racing, he exhaled slowly. He needed time to focus, to think and he couldn't do that while he was here, in Alisson, where Stacey was close by.

Friday, just before lunch, Stacey was still in her office. Since early yesterday morning, she hadn't really ventured outside of this small space. She didn't want to hear any gossip, especially not if it was about the upcoming bachelor auction.

She'd ignored all the messages and calls she'd been getting at regular intervals from Brooke, Lindsay, and Charlie. If all the sly smiles and giggles she'd received on her way to work since yesterday morning were anything to go by, Alisson's gossip mill was alive and working well, and everyone knew Jason's truck had been parked in front of her house Wednesday night.

She wasn't ready to talk about what had happened between her and Jason, though, with anyone. Damn it, it broke her heart every time she remembered the few hours they'd had together.

Love. Just four letters to describe such an all-consuming emotion. Her whole being had changed. She'd never be the same again.

Sleep had been impossible the last two nights. Even though she'd washed the bedding and aired the pillows she could still smell him, still feel those strong arms pulling her closer, still hear his heart beating below her ear as she'd lain with her head on his chest. And she could still vividly remember how ready her body had been to receive him, how perfectly she fitted against him, how astonishing it was to race up that mountain with his deep groan echoing through her body.

Grabbing a piece of paper, she used it as a fan. She was burning up, just thinking about their lovemaking. Oh, and his hands...

How could she have been so stupid to go and fall in love with him? Marriage, babies... She waited for the usual panicky feeling to grab her at the throat—but there was...nothing.

Oh, my goodness, this was why she should stay away from Jason Coleman. If she wasn't careful, she might just start dreaming about white picket fences and babies with their daddy's clear blue eyes.

Babies. Slowly, she sat down in her chair. Babies. She was thinking about babies. About Jason's babies. And she wasn't freaking out. How extraordinary!

Chewing her lip, she opened her phone. She remembered Eleanor had sent her the name of the psychologist she'd mentioned. At this point, she didn't have anything to lose—maybe it was time to get another perspective on her past.

A few minutes later, she had an appointment with Eleanor's friend in the first week of the new year.

As she sat back in her chair, someone knocked on her door. The next moment Lindsay, Charlie, and Brooke marched in. All three women had a determined glint in their eyes

Warily, she glanced up at them. "What now?"

Lindsay was the first one to speak. "Jason has left Alisson. I've just spoken to Blake."

Stacey's heart dropped to the ground. "What do you mean Jason has left Alisson? Did he go to his ranch?"

Lindsay shook her head. "I don't think so, but he's left the dojo after his two classes this morning. Said he was leaving town."

"He can't be gone. What about tomorrow night's auction?" Stacey got the words out through dry lips. What a stupid thing to say, but Jason couldn't be gone.

Brooke stepped closer and touched Stacey's arm. "Did something happen between you two. We've heard…what I mean to say is, people have been talking—"

"We've heard his truck was parked in front of your house until after midnight Wednesday night," Charlie interrupted.

"He… I…" Swallowing against a lump in her throat the size of a golf ball, Stacey tried to find words, but her mind was empty. Jason was gone—that was all she could think about. Why couldn't she breathe?

"I'll get her some water. She looks like she's ready to keel over," Lindsay whispered, then disappeared.

Charlie rushed closer. "Breathe, sweetie, breathe. I'm sure there's an ordinary explanation why he's gone."

"How do you know he's left?" Stacey managed to ask.

Lindsay was back with a bottle of water. "Drink. He's told Blake he was leaving. Didn't mention where to or for how long."

"I'm so sorry," Charlie was saying. "We don't know what happened…"

"We've made love," Stacey cried out. "That's what happened. And then I realized I've gone and fallen in love with him even though I know he's not interested in anything permanent. I wasn't interested in anything permanent either until…but then he kissed me and I…" Inhaling deeply, she wiped her eyes. "I fell for him. I thought I could explain the crazy feelings inside of me as just biology, but what I feel when I'm with him isn't something that will ever change."

"So does he know how you feel?" Brooke asked.

"No, of course not. I told him I can't see him again…"

"Oh, sweetie." Lindsay sighed, patting Stacey's arm.

"I can't see him again," Stacey cried. "I can't bear to be

with him just short-term. It'll break my heart when he leaves and I know he will leave eventually."

Charlie cocked her head. "So because you've fallen in love with Jason, you've changed your mind about having a relationship?"

"Yes, but…"

"Maybe he has too," Lindsay added.

"But he's left!" Stacey cried out.

"Well, I've come to know Jason over the past year," Lindsay said. "He's been a good friend to Blake. He'll be at the auction, I'm sure. Question is, what are you going to do about it?"

"What do you mean?"

"Oh, my goodness," Brooke laughed. "You are distracted. I'm talking about the auction?"

"But Jason's gone—he won't even be here!"

"Okay, sweetie, let's focus on what we do know," Charlie said as the three women grabbed chairs and drew them forward, sitting knee to knee with Stacey. "Jason will not let anyone down, I'm sure of it. So let's talk about how you're going to make sure no one else gets him tomorrow night."

Brooke was frowning. She'd picked up one of the booklets Stacey had made with the details of all the bachelors and was looking through it. "Why do you have Guy Richard's info in this booklet?"

Stacey rubbed her temple where the beginnings of a headache was throbbing. "He's—"

A stunned Brooke interrupted her. "Is he…? Don't tell me he's also taking part in the auction?"

Sighing, Stacey nodded. "But you can't tell anyone! I've promised to keep it a secret. He'd doing it for Eleanor."

Brooke smiled slowly. "Well, well, well. Good for Guy! I didn't think he had it in him. Wait 'til…"

"No, you're not to tell your mom before tomorrow night," Stacey repeated.

"Okay." Brooke nodded. "Not a word until tomorrow

107

night. But I am going to make sure she bids on him. I don't know what her problem is—she's always been mad about him. Until the night of our wedding when he was her date. Afterward, she refused to take any calls from him."

"Okay, ladies. It would seem we're going to be busy tomorrow night." Charlie grinned. "We need a plan."

Lindsay held up two fingers. "Two plans, I think."

CHAPTER 13

When Jason had left Alisson around lunch on Friday, he had no clear idea of where he was going. He'd just stepped on the pedal. In Livingston, he'd stopped to get gas, grab something to eat and drink before he'd left, driving south with no clear idea of where he was going.

He'd thought to maybe do some fly-fishing but that would have meant he'd have to go to the ranch, do more explaining—none of which he was in the mood for. That was also the reason he was driving Maggie and not his new truck. But so far, she was behaving herself.

Leaning forward, he saw he'd ended up on the Paradise Valley Scenic Loop, a sixty-two-mile drive that circled through the valley. He'd been meaning to explore this part of Montana anyway, but there never seemed to be time.

For miles he just drove, emptying his mind, trying to focus on the beautiful scenery. The Yellowstone River flowed through the middle of the valley, flanked by the towering peaks of the Absaroka Range to the east and the Gallatin Range to the west. Apparently, the traffic was quite heavy during the summer months, he'd been told at the gas station, but in winter the road wasn't that busy.

At some point he saw directions that would take him to

the US Highway 89, but he ignored it and continued driving the loop. He'd stopped a few times to drink in the scenery. The views were breathtaking, but his mind was so consumed with Stacey, he barely registered what he was seeing.

The next time he saw directions back toward Livingston, he pulled off the road again and got out of his truck. The sun was dipping low, the shadows getting longer. He should probably head back. But the storm brewing inside of him was keeping him on edge. Huddling in his jacket, he moved to the front of his truck. It was bitterly cold but this freezing, crisp air was exactly what he needed to clear his mind.

He'd been with women before, beautiful women, nice women, sexy women, but no one had left him feeling like this before—restless, agitated, aching.

Usually, he was the one who needed to explain why he couldn't stay, why he wouldn't be visiting again. This time 'round, Stacey was the one who'd told him she didn't want to see him again.

Pacing up and down in front of his truck, he looked up at the spectacular beauty of the surrounding mountains every now and again, but his mind didn't really take in what he saw. Stacey's features were front and center in his mind; she was all that he could see.

He remembered every single minute of the time they'd been together. The way her eyes had darkened when he'd slipped into her, the way her body had simply melted against him, the way she'd look at him as if she...as if she loved him.

His breath left his body in one whoosh, and he froze. And then he knew—damn it, of course she loved him. She wouldn't have been with him if she hadn't.

That was why she'd sent him away: she was trying to protect herself. Because he'd been very clear about not ever getting married. He even had a reason—the fact that his dad had walked out on him and his mother.

Her fear of commitment, of babies, he could understand so well, but he also knew he could help her get over it because… He tried to inhale, but his body was way too small to accommodate everything he was feeling.

Barking out a laugh, he leaned forward, his hands on his knees. Because he loved her. He'd probably always loved her, long before he'd even seen her for the first time. He had to tell her, as soon as possible. Why the hell hadn't he realized earlier how he really felt about Stacey?

Turning on his heel, he hurried back to his truck. "Okay, Maggie, sweetheart," he crooned as he patted the dashboard of his truck after he'd climbed in. "Now is not the time to get into a huff. We need to get to Alisson as soon as possible." He turned the key, but there was nothing. Not even a splutter.

Damn it to hell. Muttering and swearing, he took out his mobile. The damn battery was flat. He'd been an FBI agent, damn it, he should've known to be prepared before he went anywhere. Because he'd been so stupid and didn't realize the craziness inside him meant he'd fallen in love with Stacey, he'd left town, making every possible rookie mistake in the book—he hadn't been prepared, he hadn't made sure his phone was charged, he hadn't told anyone where he was going and he'd taken Maggie, an unreliable vehicle.

He could try to bum a lift with the first car or truck that came this way.

Fifteen minutes later, he was still waiting. It was winter, it was nearly dark—chances were nobody else was using this road today.

Cussing a blue streak, he opened the hood of the truck. He was no mechanic, but he'd watched his grandpa tinker with Maggie a few times. Maybe he could figure out what the problem was.

It was quickly getting dark, though, and there wasn't much light left.

The morning of the auction, Stacey was in her shop just after sunrise to pick up the menus Eleanor wanted. Sleep had again evaded her the previous night. She'd asked Lindsay to let her know the moment Blake heard from Jason but so far, she'd only had a text from Eleanor asking her if she would mind helping at the town hall that morning.

She'd been so grateful to have something to do, she hadn't even minded Eleanor's assumption that she'd just drop everything to run to her aid.

Hopefully, she'd be kept so busy today, she wouldn't have time to worry about Jason.

As soon had the thought entered her mind or she was worrying again. Had he taken his new truck or was he driving Maggie? How stupid could you be? Surely, he would've known not to take the dilapidated vehicle on the road? Oh, but he loved that truck. He could be stuck anywhere: nobody even had any idea in which direction he went. And 'round and 'round her mind went.

Oh, damn it, this was driving her crazy. Would Jason even make it to the auction that night? What if something seriously bad had happened to him? What if…?

Inhaling deeply, she picked up the box with the menus of the bachelors. Jason was a grown man. He'd probably decided to go away for a few days. There was no reason for him to tell anyone about his plans. He worked with Blake, so at some point he'd probably send a message to let him know when he'd be back.

Until then, she had work to do. She'd be so happy when this freaking auction was done. With all the extra things she had to do for Eleanor, she'd fallen behind with her other work. Hopefully things would return to normal next week.

Normal? Her life had changed forever. Nothing would be normal again. She'd fallen in love and that had changed everything, had changed her.

She struggled to keep her mind on what she was supposed to do, so that it took her much longer to carry the boxes, projector, and computer out to her car than it was supposed to. There was a projector in the town hall, but from previous experience she knew it didn't always work.

When she finally locked her shop and walked toward her car, it was mid-morning. As she neared her car, a truck coming down the street, stopped next to her. Blake was behind the wheel.

"Uhm...everything okay?" she asked with her heart in her throat.

"We've just heard from Blake, he..."

"Is he okay?" she interrupted before he could finish.

Blake nodded. "His truck finally up and died, and his mobile hadn't been charged. Apparently, he was able to fix that pile of steel he calls a truck and made it back to Livingston, where he spent the rest of the night. The truck refused to move another inch when he got there, so he had no other option. He phoned me from someone else's phone."

Lightheaded, Stacey leaned against her car, her legs strangely heavy. "Okay...okay, thanks," she got out.

"Stacey? You okay?" Blake asked, frowning. "You're white as a sheet."

"I'm... I'm fine," she said, and quickly got into her car.

"We'll see you later tonight," Blake called out as he drove off.

Jason was fine. Overwhelmed with relief, she dropped her head to the steering wheel. What if something had happened to him and she hadn't had a chance to tell him she loved him? Could she tell him, though? Knowing how he felt about marriage—could she be that brave?

He'd accused her of being a coward, and maybe he was right. If she told him she loved him without knowing if he felt the same way, she'd be putting everything on the line. Could she do that?

Her phone bleeped. It was Eleanor, asking whether she was on her way.

She quickly started her car and drove own Main Road toward the town hall. Seconds later, she realized she still had a stupid smile on her face. Jason was safe. And she was going to see him tonight.

For the first time, she remembered again: Jason was one of the bachelors. Oh, my. Lindsay, Charlie, and Brooke had spoken about plans, but she hadn't really paid attention. She'd been too worried about Jason. Besides, there was no way she'd be able to bid on Jason or anyone else. She was just too shy.

The pesky little voice was back, though. And what if Sandy Rivers bid on him?

Aargh, she wasn't going to think about that now. She had work to do.

As she stopped in front of the town hall, Eleanor rushed out, hands in the air, her face flushed from all the excitement. "Oh, Stacey, they tell me Jason is fine! I'm so happy to hear that. Have you brought——"

Stacey picked up the box from her car. "Got it. What do you want me to do?"

"They're building a catwalk for the men to strut their stuff," Eleanor said.

"A catwalk?" Stacey asked, surprised.

"Yes, dear, we're trying to be very professional," Eleanor huffed as they entered the hall.

Biting her cheeks so she didn't laugh, Stacey stared in amazement at the activity in front of her. It seemed the whole of Alisson had been summoned to help with the event. She recognized a few teachers, most of the ranchers and ranch hands around town, and just about every shop owner.

"You have been busy." She chuckled.

"It's for a good cause," Eleanor said. "Surely you can tell me now who bachelor number ten is?"

"Sorry, I promised to keep it a secret until the very end.

What do you want me to do?" she added quickly before Eleanor could pin her down with one of her stares. She wasn't immune to those.

It had taken forever to get a breakdown truck willing to tow Maggie home. In the end, Jason had to settle for someone who was only able to do it on Monday.

By the time he'd paid and left directions to deliver Maggie to the ranch, it was mid-afternoon.

"We'd better hurry," Blake said and they drove away from Livingston, "Eleanor will have my hide if you're late."

"Does…does everyone know I was gone?"

Laughing, Blake slapped him on the shoulder. "If you want to know whether Stacey knows, just ask."

"Okay, damn it, does she know?"

"Last time we saw her, she was white as a sheet when I told her your sorry ass was fine," Blake said. "We were all worried about you. Of all the stupid things…"

"I know, okay. I know. I…had to clear my head."

"And?" Blake asked.

"What do you mean?" Jason frowned.

Blake smiled. "Have you cleared your head?"

Rubbing his face, Jason nodded. "Yeah. Turns out I… I've fallen for her."

There was a brief silence in the truck.

"About damn time you realize it." Blake finally chuckled and slapped him on the shoulder. There was obviously no need to explain who was the "her" he was talking about. "Took you long enough. Does that mean we're having another wedding soon?"

Jason shook his head. "I don't think so. She's always been very adamant about not getting married or having babies."

"I'm married to one," Blake began, "but I'm the last man to tell you I understand women. What I have learned, though, is do what your gut tells you to do. And be very clear about your feelings. Spell it out. Don't think they know because even if they do know, they still want to talk about feelings."

"Feelings?"

Blake nodded. "Yeah. Feelings. They always want to talk about feelings."

Jason shook his head. Oh, man. He'd never been good with that.

Blake finally turned into Jason's ranch and dropped him off in front of his house. "You'd better hurry. Eleanor wants you at the town hall at six sharp."

"Thanks for picking me up. I appreciate it."

"It's okay. You and me, we don't have to talk about feelings," Blake teased, before he drove away.

CHAPTER 14

Stacey stared at herself in the mirror. The last time she'd dressed up had been for Brooke and Gavin's wedding, way back in June when it was summer. She hadn't even thought of buying anything new for tonight. She was going to hand out the menus, make sure the projector was connected to her laptop to display all the info on the bachelors against a screen, and then head home. A pair of jeans and a top would do.

But when she'd opened her closet earlier, she'd picked the black velvet pants she so seldom wore and the soft blue shimmering top she'd bought a while back and had never worn yet. As she put it on over the black satin and lace underwear, she couldn't stop a grin. Jason had never seen her in anything other than jeans and a top over the last few weeks. Her hair she'd washed and left to dry in wild curls around her face.

She'd dressed for him, for his pleasure. When he saw her tonight, his eyes would darken as they did, she knew it. Inhaling shakily, she put a hand to her tummy where the butterflies were going crazy. Whether she'd have the guts to actually put up her hand and bid on Jason was still up for debate.

Her phone bleeped. It was Guy Richard wanting to know where the hell she was. Grinning, she quickly sent him a text before she grabbed her coat. It would seem she wasn't the only nervous person around tonight.

When she arrived at the town hall, she found Guy in the parking lot. He'd obviously been waiting for her and the moment she'd parked, he opened her car door.

"I… I don't think I can do this," he said.

Stacey slowly got out of her car. "That is such a pity. You look very handsome."

"I feel like a damn penguin in this get-up."

"A great looking penguin." Stacey smiled, patting his arm. "It's for a good cause, Mr. Richard…"

"Guy, please."

Stacey nodded. "Okay, Guy. We're all doing this for the kids of this town. You wouldn't begrudge someone a chance to go and study, would you?"

"No, but what if Eleanor…?"

Taking his arm, she steered him in the direction of the hall. "You leave Eleanor to us. Go out and enjoy yourself."

"Could you help me with this damn bow tie?" he asked as they neared the steps leading up to the town hall.

As she stepped forward to help him, she saw Eleanor approaching. Behind her were Charlie, Lindsay, and Brooke with their husbands.

"Eleanor," Stacey called out. "Could you help us, please? I'm sure you're much more comfortable tying a bow tie…"

Eleanor's mouth opened and closed, but she couldn't get a word out. "Guy," she finally managed.

Over Eleanor's head, Guy's somewhat stunned eyes found hers. Nodding ever so slightly, she smiled. "Great, thanks, Eleanor. You all look so nice," Stacey said as she turned toward the women.

"I don't know if I still know how to do it…" Eleanor mumbled.

"Of course, you do," Guy said, all his previous

nervousness gone. He stood perfectly still until Eleanor had finished. "Thank you, Eleanor. Will you please show me where the bachelors are supposed to wait?"

Eleanor inhaled sharply. "You mean...?"

"Meet bachelor number ten," Stacey said.

"Oh, my goodness," was all Eleanor managed.

Guy offered her his arm. "Shall we go?"

Only when the two older people had entered the hall did Brooke's giggle slip out. "Oh, that was so funny! Hopefully this'll teach her to stop meddling in other people's lives."

"What's going on?" Logan asked, frowning.

Charlie took his arm. "Your mother doesn't know it yet, but she's going to bid on Guy Richard."

"Why?" Logan asked.

"Because they should've been together long ago," Brooke said. "Mom has always put us before herself but now that we are both happily married, she should have her own life as well. Guy is smitten with her, but since our wedding she's been avoiding him."

"So are you three gals..." Logan said pointing among Lindsay, Charlie, and Brooke, "playing matchmakers?"

Grinning, Charlie leaned against her husband. "Now you get it. Come on, let's find our seats.

Just then Sandy Rivers and a group of her friends approached. Sandy's coat was open, showing off her long legs and not much else underneath. She walked toward Stacey. "Sorry for you, Stacey, but I'm determined to win the bid on Jason, just so you know."

"Hallo, Sandy," Charlie smiled. "You do look ready for battle. Good luck!"

"No luck needed." Sandy smirked.

Stacey turned away and walked blindly into the hall. She couldn't compete with the other women Jason had dated. What had she been thinking? Computer nerds like her were simply not on the same level as the likes of Sandy Rivers and her crowd.

"Stacey, wait up!" Charlie was calling from behind.

"Sorry, I'm here to help Eleanor and then I'm leaving," Stacey said.

Brooke took her one arm and Charlie the other one. "Nonsense," Charlie said. "Of course you're not leaving. We are here to support the kids, remember? And we must make sure Eleanor wins the bid on Guy."

"My mom has a competitive streak. I'm not worried." Brooke laughed. "I've asked a number of her friends to bid on Guy. She's not going to like that."

Shaking his head, Gavin took Brooke's arm. "She's going to make sure she wins."

"I know!" Brooke laughed. "It will probably a lesson for her not to interfere in other people's lives."

"I am very grateful for your mother's interference. After all, I got you out of the deal," Gavin said, bending down to kiss his wife.

Stacey swallowed down the sudden lump in her throat. Oh, my goodness, she was getting tearful watching a couple kiss. This was probably what being in love did to a person.

Just then, a wide-eyed Billie rushed closer. "Stacey, we're struggling with the projector and screen. Eleanor is freaking out. I'm worried she'll burst something."

Stacey quickly followed Billie. Fixing electronic problems she could do—dealing with her feelings, not so much.

The flutter of butterflies on her tummy was going crazy. Any minute now, she'd probably see Jason.

A haggard-looking Eleanor rushed forward as Stacey neared the table where the projector was. "Stacey, my dear. There are so many problems, I don't know where to start. Could you fix this projector and then go and help in the dressing room, please? Some of our bachelors are apparently struggling with their bow ties."

"Oh, but I'm not the right person—" Stacey began.

Eleanor had turned away already. "You'll be doing me

such a favor. Thank you, my dear," she called over her shoulder.

Seriously, why couldn't grown men dress themselves? Muttering, Stacey bent down to check what the problem was. With a sigh, she noticed immediately what was wrong—someone had switched it off. Seriously.

The butterflies on her tummy went wild. Now she had to go to the dressing room. Behind the stage. Where the bachelors were waiting.

The possibility that she'd see Jason when she went behind the curtains was becoming intensely real.

Jason parked his truck behind the town hall and slipped in through the back door. He really didn't feel comfortable strutting around wearing this damn penguin suit.

Most of the other men he'd seen that day in Stacey's shop were already there, joking and trying their best—and most of them failing—to look unconcerned and cool about what was about to happen.

Guy Richard, the attorney who'd helped him when he'd bought the ranch, was also there, dressed in a tux and looking even more uncomfortable than anyone else.

"Guy!" he called out. "Don't tell me Eleanor managed to rope you in as well?"

"She didn't know I'd be here until a few minutes ago. I've arranged it with Stacey. When a woman keeps ignoring your calls, you do what you have to do to make sure she notices you," he said, fiddling with his bow tie.

"I'll be rooting for you." Jason tried to calm the older man down.

Just then, Eleanor rushed in, looking all flustered. "Jason, sweetie, I need you in the dressing room, please. Just through there. I'll be with you in a mo."

Frowning, he turned away and walked toward the dressing room. Why would Eleanor want him in the dressing room? Like everyone else, he'd arrived already dressed.

As he opened the door, the redhead who was inside turned around and her eyes widened. His heart kicked in his ribs. It was Stacey, looking heartbreakingly beautiful.

For a millisecond, he couldn't believe his eyes. She was actually here. Right in front of him. *Thank you, Eleanor.*

She exhaled slowly. "How did you know—?"

"You'd be here? I didn't. Eleanor—"

Stace smiled tremulously. "Of course. I'm sorry she'd wasted your—"

With two steps he covered the short distance between them. "I can't tell you how happy I am to see you. I thought I'd have to wait the whole freaking night before we could talk." Picking up her hands, he lifted her arms. "Just look at you. You're gorgeous," he muttered as looked his fill.

"Are you okay? I heard you were gone and I didn't know... I was worried you wouldn't be back." There was a light in those blue eyes he'd never seen there before.

Cupping her face with unsteady hands, he stared into her eyes, hoping she could see in his what she meant to him. Talk about your feelings, Blake had said, but he'd never been good with that. And now that so much was riding on mere words, he was worried not finding the exact ones she needed to hear.

"Ladies and the few gentlemen who are brave enough to be here," Coach McNeally's voice boomed over the loudspeakers. "Please take your seats. We are about to start with the auction."

Well, he only had a few more seconds: he was going for broke. As it was, he'd wasted enough time already. "Stace, I have a confession to make."

A shadow dropped over her eyes. "I know about all the women you've dated over the past week."

"You told me to do it, remember? And I thought—stupidly—maybe it's not a bad idea. But you know what happened?"

With those blue eyes never leaving his face, she shook her head.

"I realized I don't want to be with anybody else but you."

Those gorgeous eyes darkened just the way he remembered. "Jason..."

"If everyone is ready?" Coach McNeally's voice rose above the noise in the hall.

"Damn it, there isn't time to talk right now. I want to see you tonight, after the auction, please?" he pleaded.

"Where is everybody?" Eleanor's slightly hysterical voice called from somewhere close.

"This damn circus," he muttered, and pulled Stacey closer. "I have to go, but I—" And inhaling her scent, he kissed her.

Her mouth softened, silky arms crept around his neck, and with a groan, he stepped in between her legs, cupping her breasts with his hands.

A loud knock on the door and a frantic voice finally penetrated his befuddled brain. He lifted his head. Stacey's lips were swollen from their kiss, her eyes darkened with passion.

"Bid on me, please?" he asked, playing with one of her hardened nipples. "I don't want to be with anyone else but you."

"I don't know..."

"Damn it, Stace!"

"I'll try."

"Yeah." "I can't wait," he murmured as he quickly bent down to drop another kiss on her lips.

"Jason!" someone called.

"Remind me to thank Eleanor for arranging this meeting," he said. With a last look at her, he opened the door and left. There was so much he needed to tell her, but it would have to wait until after this freaking auction.

Stacey sagged down on the closest chair. Oh, my. Could she believe what she'd just seen in Jason's eyes? Hunger, desire, and something else that had never been so obvious. Could it be…?

Inhaling deeply, she touched her lips, still throbbing from Jason's kiss. Her breasts were heavy in anticipation of his touch. But trying to guess what was going on in a man's mind was probably not a good idea.

She should've figured Eleanor would pull some or other stunt like this. But she couldn't be angry with the older woman. Finding Jason in the dressing room had been the best surprise of the night.

He wanted to see her later. She had no idea why and she didn't really care. Whether he wanted to be with her for a day or a week or a month, she was going to agree to whatever terms he had.

She loved him and she wanted to spend every possible moment with him. Even if it was only for a little while. All of her past fears seemed to have vanished since the moment she'd realized she loved him.

Her phoned bleeped. It was Billie. She was needed in the hall. Inhaling shakily, she put a hand on her tummy where the butterflies were going wild.

Oh, my.

CHAPTER 15

As Jason joined the other bachelors, a flustered-looking Eleanor rushed closer. "You've been to the dressing room?" she asked him softly.

Grinning, Jason nodded. "Oh, yes, thank you. I owe you big time."

"You two belong together. Don't know why it took you so long to figure it out." With a wink, she turned to the other men. "Okay everyone, look over here, please?" She motioned to a big whiteboard in the corner. "Your names as you'll appear on stage. You go on one by one, strut your stuff down the catwalk while Coach McNeally tells the ladies more about you.

"As you walk around, the ladies will start bidding. Once everyone is done, you all line up again in front of the curtain at the end, to give a final wave to everyone. For those of you who have never done this before, I must warn you. It gets wild out there. Just grin and remember we're all here because we're trying to help the kids of this town."

As she turned to rush away, Guy swiftly moved in front of her. "Eleanor…"

"Not…not now, Guy," she stammered and quickly

moved away.

With a determined glint in his eye, Guy stared after her, clearly not deterred by Eleanor's manner.

Jason moved to the heavy curtains and peeked through a slit. The place was filled with women of all sizes and ages. He scanned over the crowd until he saw Stacey. She was right at the back of the hall, busy with a projector.

She was always beautiful, never mind what clothes she wore, but tonight, in the blue shimmering top that moved with her as it caught the lights, she was breathtaking. His fingers itched as his eyes slid over that gorgeous red hair falling down her back. He couldn't wait for this circus to finish so that he could have her all to himself.

Just then she looked up, straight to where he was standing. She couldn't possibly see him, but she had to have sensed he was watching her.

Someone touched him from behind and he turned around. It was Tripp Young, the leader of the band who was playing tonight.

"You wanted to see me?" he asked.

"Yeah. I have a favor to ask…"

By the time Jason had finished explaining, Tripp was grinning. "Any time. Until later, man."

Jason exhaled slowly. He didn't know whether he was going to win the bet he'd had with Stacey, but he was going all-out tonight to win her heart.

The drummer of the band set up at the side of the stage eventually brought down the noise level with a roll of his drums. Over the last few minutes, the estrogen level had noticeably risen; the air was heavy with anticipation.

When Coach McNeally appeared from behind the curtains, a roar went up. "Ladies and…I see two gentlemen, no—Bob Bates makes three! Welcome to this fundraiser." Just a few house rules…"

"Ooh, I can't wait!" Billie giggled as Coach McNeally

explained how the night would progress. She was clutching Stacey's arm, her face flushed with excitement. "I wonder when Stone…"

"We ask that you please stay in your seats during the performance. Okay, ladies, let's get this show on the road. The first bachelor up is Stone Warner."

As Coach McNeally shouted details about Stone over the microphone, the crowd went wild. The noise was deafening. Everyone leaped from their chairs. Billie was also jumping up and down, punching her fist in the air. Even the older ladies from Eleanor's bridge club, sitting predatorily in the front row, were on their feet. Obviously, no one was paying any heed to Coach's request.

"Look at this bachelor's info behind me on the screen. You also have his details with you. What do you say, shall we start the bidding at one hundred dollars? Do I have a hundred?"

Hands went up, voices rose. Billie rushed forward to the catwalk, followed by most of the women.

"Ladies, seats please!" Coach McNeally tried, but he was flatly ignored.

Everyone seemed to be jumping up and down. Hands waved money in the air; the women went wild. *Wow.* Stacey laughed. She'd never seen anything like this. Even the shyest of women were letting down their hair tonight.

"I have a hundred and forty from the woman in the pink," he called out, pointing toward Billie.

"Hundred and fifty!" another voice shouted.

Immediately, Billie's hand shot up again. "Two hundred!"

Stacey gulped. Billie was clearly determined to win her man.

"Going for the third time," Coach McNeally called out, pointing at Billie, "you, young lady, have won a date with Stone Warner!"

Billie was grinning from ear to ear when she returned. Screaming and shouting, her friends all congratulated her."

"You won't mind giving me an advance, will you?" Billie mouthed to Stacey above the noise.

Stacey just smiled and nodded.

One by one, the bachelors strutted their stuff. The local vet, Roger O'Connor, was obviously enjoying the whole thing. His shirt was unbuttoned after the first round and when the bidding reached two hundred and fifty dollars, he removed it completely, at which point the crowd nearly brought down the hall.

A grinning Dottie Hanson, Eleanor's friend, won the bid at a three hundred dollars.

Coach McNeally tapped on the microphone. "Okay, ladies, we have two more gentlemen for you. Up next, we have the surprise bachelor. Just to show you, age doesn't matter. This time the bidding will start at three hundred dollars. Experience doesn't come cheap!"

As Guy walked out, the crowd went ballistic. Stacey tried to see where Eleanor was, but everyone was now in front, jumping up and down and chanting Guy's name.

"We have three hundred and fifty from the seriously sexy woman in red in the front!" The coach could barely be heard above the noise. "Come on, ladies, this is an experienced bachelor, show him your appreciation. What about three eighty? Anyone bidding three eighty?"

Stacey was still trying to figure out who the woman was who had bid on Guy when another hand shot up.

"And we have four hundred!" Coach McNeally cried. "Four hundred, ladies. Surely you can do better than a measly four hundred dollars, what about four-fifty? Do I have four-fifty? This bachelor could show you a seriously good time…"

"Five hundred!" a voice cried out and the noise level rose another few decibels.

"Okay, five hundred for the lady in red, going once, going twice…"

"Eight hundred!" a voice shouted from behind her.

Gasping, Stacey turned around. It was Eleanor. Hands

on her hips, her chin stuck out, it was clear she was in a fighting mood. She was going to win this bid.

Guy strode—nearly strutted—down the catwalk, his eyes on Eleanor. As he reached the end, he held out his hand toward her.

Eleanor blinked, clearly rattled about what had happened. The next moment, Brooke was at her side, taking her arm and gently leading her toward Guy. Guy came down the stairs, took Eleanor's hand and pulled her close. Under loud clapping and yelling, he kissed her before he led her back up the stairs and pulled her behind the curtains with him.

It took a long time for the crowd to settle down. The noise level rose even further. It was clear the ladies of Alisson were now really into this bidding thing.

The only bachelor who still had to make an appearance was Jason. Her heart hammering away, Stacey looked around her. Diagonally in front of her, Sandy was standing on a chair, obviously geared to bid on Jason.

She looked at the exit. Maybe she should just go. Nobody would notice her if she slipped away now. But she had promised Jason she would try to bid on him. She was a shuddering mess. She didn't know whether she could do this.

A movement to her right drew her attention. A very determined-looking Brooke, Charlie, and Lindsay were on their way to her. Sighing, she shook her head. Her friends were clearly on a mission to make sure she bid on Jason.

"Now it's Jason's turn," Brooke said. "You are going to bid on him and you are going to win."

"Oh, Brooke, I don't know. I'm no good at this kind of thing…"

"Nonsense," Lindsay said. "It's fun."

"Where are your husbands? Shouldn't you be with them?" she tried.

"They escaped a while ago." Brooke winked. "They're waiting for us in the foyer, at the bar."

"And last but not least," Coach McNeally was saying. "We have Jason Coleman. At six feet two inches, his physique *speaks* for itself. See what I did there, ladies?"

Jason walked on to the stage as the coach continued talking about him. The noise level rose, women whistled, yelled, went crazy. As Jason sauntered down the catwalk, he was smiling, looking directly at Stacey. Her heart just about leapt out of her body.

"We'll start the bidding at a hundred…"

"Two hundred!" a voice yelled even before Coach had finished speaking.

"It's Sandy," Brooke muttered, pointing to where the brunette was jumping up and down on her chair.

"We have two hundred…" Coach McNeally said.

"Three hundred!" Sandy yelled before Stacey could even lift her hand.

Jason grimaced before he turned and walked back toward the curtains.

"Five hundred!" Sandy screamed again, not giving anyone else a chance to bid.

Coach McNeally was rubbing his neck. "We have five hundred dollars, ladies. Anyone else?"

"Six hundred!" Sandy yelled, waving money in the air.

Stacey was so stunned, she dropped the hand she'd nearly had in the air.

Another hand rose right in the front of the hall. "A thousand dollars!"

A collective gasp went up in the crowd. Coach McNeally laughed. "We have a thousand dollars to the lady in red in the front. Going once…"

"Oh, my goodness, it's Dottie Hanson again!" Charlie laughed. "Stacey? You seriously have to do something…"

"Going to the lady in red!" Coach McNeally shouted.

Jason was frowning as he looked at Stacey.

The crowd erupted. Under loud shouts and yelling, all the bachelors appeared in front of the curtain again, bowing to the crowd. Amid more clapping and cheering,

Coach McNeally explained how the paying and the dating would work before the bachelors left the stage.

Nobody was in a hurry to go anywhere, and everyone lingered in the hall. The excitement hadn't died down yet.

A clearly disappointed Sandy walked past Stacey. "It's ridiculous for such an old biddy to think someone like Jason would want to take her anywhere," she announced to everyone around.

"You were free to bid more, young lady." Dottie Hanson snorted behind her. "A pity you didn't have the money."

Sandy looked ready to explode.

"Just a minute, everyone," Coach McNeally called out before Sandy could say anything. "There is a surprise for one of you ladies. Apparently, the person who the surprise is for will know who she is. Don't move," Coach said, before he disappeared behind the curtains.

The first notes of a well-known love song filled the town hall; everyone immediately fell silent. A lone figure pulled the curtains aside and walked out on to the stage with a guitar in hand.

Stacey lost all her breath. It was Jason. In the huge crowd his gaze found hers.

I'll never not love you...

Keeping his gaze only on her, he walked down the catwalk, singing. He'd remembered the bet she'd made with him. What she couldn't have foreseen was that he had a beautiful voice. The man could really sing.

"Aaah—this is the bet you guys had, isn't it?" Brooke asked, smiling. "He's got a great voice, did you know?"

Her eyes on him, Stacey shook her head. "I had no idea."

"I bet Blake knows," Lindsay said. "But he didn't say anything."

She was taking a step toward Jason when Sandy came rushing past them, her eyes on Jason. "It's our song!" she yelled. "Oh, Jason!" She leaped on to the stage and ran down the catwalk to where Jason was standing.

Stunned, Stacey turned around quickly and made for the door. This, she couldn't watch. Oh, my goodness, she'd probably misunderstood what Jason had said. But— but he'd kissed her... It obviously hadn't meant anything...

Tears were running down her cheeks as she ran toward the parking lot. Fortunately, everyone else was still inside the hall and she was able to get into her car and speed away without having to wait for traffic.

She was shivering so much, it was difficult to see the road in front of her. It had also started to rain. The spot where her heart was supposed to be, was just a big hole.

Sniffling, she slowed down her car. Her house was just around the next corner, she was nearly there.

As she took the turn, something darted across the road and she swerved away, trying not to hit whatever it was. The car spun around, and helpless, she watched in horror as she skidded toward a lamp pole. Nothing she tried worked, and bracing herself, she watched resignedly as her car slid forward toward the pole.

I haven't told Jason how she felt about him. It was her last thought before a blackness engulfed her.

CHAPTER 16

With his gaze trained on the back of the hall where Stacey had just disappeared, Jason forcefully pulled Sandy's hands from around his neck. Damn it to hell. Not even trying to sing to Stacey had gone according to plan.

"Oh, Jason!" Sandy was still saying over and over.

He hadn't wanted to be rude, but this was getting more and more ridiculous by the minute. "Sandy, seriously. The song wasn't for you, it was for—"

Sandy's eyes narrowed. "But you dated me—"

"No, I haven't. I took you on one date and I shouldn't have. I'm in love with Stacey. I'm sorry if you got the wrong idea. Please excuse me." Without looking back, he jumped from the catwalk and raced out of the hall.

Stacey wasn't outside. Neither were any of her friends. He'd seen her with Brooke, Charlie, Lindsay, and their husbands. Dejected, he walked toward his truck. Damn it to hell, why hadn't she waited for him? He'd told her he wanted to talk to her, told her he wanted to see her. He'd kissed her, for crying out loud, and there was no doubt: she'd kissed him back.

His gaze had been fixed on Stacey and he was so sure she was on her way to him, but then she'd simply turned around and rushed out. Because of freaking Sandy Rivers.

He hadn't even realized Sandy was on stage until she'd thrown her arms around him, shouting that he was singing the song for her.

Glumly, he got into his truck. This love business was way too complicated for him. He'd go and have a beer at the bar before heading back to his ranch.

Five minutes later, he was in the bar. The place was just about empty. Most folks were probably still over at the town hall. He noticed Tod and Larry behind the bar and walked toward them. They'd had to have also just arrived; they'd been selling drinks at the hall during the auction.

"Taken to the hospital, I believe," Larry was telling Tod.

Tod shook his head. "I hope she's okay. Looking at the wreck her car is, it's difficult to believe she got out alive."

"Was someone in an accident?" Jason asked as he pulled up one of the chairs.

"Yes, Stacey from the printing shop. You should know her. Haven't you brought her here for dinner recently? Heaven knows what happened, but her car..."

The words exploded in his mind. Before Tod had finished his sentence, Jason was halfway to the door. *Stacey. Accident.* He was struggling to breathe. What if she was badly hurt? What if...? He had to get to her as soon as possible.

If anything happened to her...

Outside, he sprinted toward his truck.

Stacey swung her legs off the bed. She was getting out of here. She'd been prodded and poked enough for one night, thank you very much.

The curtains around the bed in the ER opened for the umpteenth time and irritated, she looked up. But it wasn't another member of the hospital staff, thank goodness. A worried-looking Brooke, Charlie, and Lindsay rushed in.

"We saw your car on the side of the road," Charlie called out.

"Are you okay?" Brooke asked, touching Stacey's arm.

"Oh, sweetie," Lindsay sniffled, "we had such a fright when we saw your car looking like that. Are you really okay?"

Stacey put her feet slowly on the ground. She was still feeling a bit woozy, but she definitely wasn't staying in this madhouse. "I'm fine. I'll probably be black and blue by tomorrow, but fortunately nothing broke—"

"Where the hell is Stacey Lawrence?" a voice bellowed from the other side of the curtain.

Stacey's head whipped up.

It was Jason. "No, I refused to wait in the waiting room. She's... I have to see her. Now!"

Brooke opened the curtain. "Jason, stop yelling, she's here."

"Is she...?" Stacey heard his voice broke before the curtain opened again. A pale Jason stepped inside the cubicle. "Stacey..." he breathed, before he lifted her off her feet and cradled her close.

His whole body was shuddering and with a groan, he buried his face in her neck. "Stacey, sweetheart, you're okay," he repeated over and over, holding her even tighter.

"Well, I think our job here is done." Charlie laughed.

"You need any help with Stacey?" Brooke asked.

Jason lifted his head and looked down at Stacey. "It depends on her. Will you come home with me?"

"What about Sandy?"

Jason's expletive was short. "Damn it, woman, I sang that song for you. What's more, you know it. I was looking directly at you. You either believe me or you don't. Are you coming home with me?"

With her heart just about jumping out of her chest, she cocked her head. "I'm sorry, I can't," she said.

This time he put her down quickly. "In that case, I won't bother you again." Lips pressed tightly together, he turned away.

"I need to pick up a few things from my house first," she said to his retreating back.

He was about the pull open the curtains, but his hands froze.

"We'll see you tomorrow," Charlie sang, as she and Brooke and Lindsay quickly exited the small cubicle.

But Stacey barely registered her friends' exit. Her gaze was on Jason.

Slowly he turned around. His eyes were mere slits, the muscles in his cheeks working overtime. "I'm too raw to play games tonight, Stace. I died a thousand deaths thinking you could be hurt, or worse."

"I'm really fine and I'd love to come home with you," she said.

"Are you sure? Because you see," he said as he stepped closer, "once you're on the ranch, I don't know if I'll ever be able to let you go again."

Slipping her arms around his neck, she pulled him as close as her bruised ribs would allow. "Well then, I'll be there as long as you want me."

"Oh, I'll always want you," he breathed, before his lips found hers again.

Sinking into the kiss, she leaned against him. The dull ache in her heart she was going to ignore. There would be enough time for crying once his dopamine and norepinephrine levels went down and he was done with her.

A week later, Stacey parked the rental car she'd been driving since the accident in front of her house. She'd just finished for the day but before she could drive out to Jason's ranch, she had to get more clothes and the few plants in her house needed water.

Hopefully, the payout of her wrecked car's insurance would come through quickly: she needed to buy another car. She still freaked out a little bit when she remembered the state of her poor vehicle after the accident. How she got out alive was anyone's guess.

At least the huge bump on her forehead had paled to a sickly yellow, and the swelling was down. She wasn't feeling herself, though. Since the accident, she'd been lethargic, without energy, and staying awake after lunch was fast becoming a problem.

It couldn't be anything serious. They'd done what had felt like a thousand tests on her while she was in the ER, but maybe she was coming down with something. She smiled. It was most probably due to a serious lack of sleep. Since she'd moved in with Jason, sleep hadn't been a priority.

As she closed the front door, she looked around her. This had been her home, her safe space, the place where she'd been in control, but that was before she'd fallen in love. Now it was just another house, a building. The difference was Jason. He wasn't here.

In her room, she took down another suitcase from her closet. She had no idea how long this idyllic situation was going to last and she wasn't asking any questions. It wasn't forever, she knew that. Her eyes were wide open, but she was making the most of every minute she was spending with Jason.

Yawning, she started packing. Goodness, she was so sleepy. Somehow, she'd have to try and get more shut-eye.

Jason was an insatiable lover and, she'd discovered, so was she. Whenever she turned around in bed at night or when he moved, they reached out for one another. And oh, the heat, the immediate glorious heat between them wasn't something she'd ever get used to.

What the man could do with his hands…

Her phone rang. It was Jason.

"Hey, you," she said.

"I'm here and you're not," he said, not hiding the fact he wasn't pleased.

"I had to pick up more clothes. I'm leaving now."

"I can't wait to see you, but please drive carefully?"

"I will."

"Stace?"

Her breath got stuck in the throat. "Yeah?"

"We seriously have to talk, okay?"

Exhaling softly, she swallowed. "I know. On my way." Quickly, she threw some clothes in the suitcase before she headed outside.

Jason kept saying they had to talk, but that was the last thing she wanted to do. Talking would end this idyllic situation. Up until now, she'd been able to stop him from having a serious conversation him by simply kissing him, but sooner or later he was going to want to sit down and explain the situation to her. He'd want to make sure she knew this was only temporary.

Damn it, she knew that, but if she could postpone the conversation for just a little while longer, she'd do it.

Friday evening, nearly two weeks after Stacey's accident, Jason stopped his truck in front of the homestead on his ranch and jumped out.

Thank goodness, he'd just fulfilled his obligation for the bachelor auction. He couldn't be happier it was behind him. Fortunately, Dottie Hanson was very happy when he suggested they go for coffee. He'd asked Stacey to join them, but she'd gravely told him she couldn't spoil Dottie's fun like that. He'd seen her eyes twinkle, though. She liked to tease him, all right.

It was the last Friday of December. The weather was steadily getting worse. He was pleased to see Stacey's rental car was already parked in the driveway. His heart constricted like it did every time he thought of the way her vehicle had looked after the accident.

He still couldn't believe anyone got out of that wreck alive. She was getting another car as soon as the insurance money paid out, she'd told him. What he really wanted to do was buy her a big car, one that wouldn't fold up like her small car had in the accident, but by now he knew exactly how independent she could be.

Even though Stacey had been living with him for nearly two weeks already, he still couldn't believe she was actually here, in his house, on his ranch. He'd never really thought about what it meant to be happy, to be content, but over the past fourteen days he'd come to understand what pure joy meant.

When he'd bought his ranch outside Alisson, he'd reckoned being the owner of a piece of land would be the ultimate kick. And it was, but it didn't come close to what he felt when he got home and saw Stacey's car in the driveway.

Being with her, living with her, making love to her… He was a very lucky man. And every night he got home, he had plans to discuss their future together. But then he'd walk into the kitchen. She'd be cooking and swaying those sexy hips to some tune she was listening to and he'd be a goner. Up until now, they hadn't gotten 'round to having dinner before ten at night.

Excited because he was going to see her within minutes, he sprinted up the porch stairs and opened the front door. The smell of something burning hung in the air. What the…? "Stace?" he called out, rushing toward the kitchen. "Is everything okay" Baby…?"

But the kitchen was empty except for smoke billowing upward from the direction of the oven. He quickly opened the window, grabbed the over gloves lying on top of the stove, and opened the back door.

Whatever had been in the dish she'd prepared was unrecognizable. A black piece of charcoal was all that was left. Where was Stacey? Quickly he put the dish down, then opened another window, before he raced out of the kitchen.

Stacey was so organized; she'd never let food burn.

"Stace?" he called again, and listened. From somewhere upstairs he heard a sound. Taking the stairs two at a time, his heart racing, he called her again. "Stace?"

The bedroom door was open. He rushed in, only to stop in his tracks. She was lying on her side on the bed, fast asleep, her hand tucked in under her chin.

His heart finally settled. Exhaling slowly, he sat down next to her on the bed. She looked so pale. What on earth could be wrong? "Stace, sweetheart, talk to me," he whispered, combing her hair out of her face.

Her eyes opened slowly. For a moment she stared at him, clearly not quite awake yet, but then her eyes widened and she sat upright. "The food…"

"Has burned," he finished her sentence.

"Oh, my goodness, I'm so sorry. I was just going to close my eyes for a minute, I must've… I made you a stew."

Laughing, he pulled her close to him. "You work all day. You seriously don't have to cook every night. Why don't you have a bath and I'll make dinner?"

"Let me clean up the kitchen—"

He pulled her on to his lap "I've got this. You go and have a bath."

With a sigh, she relaxed against him. Pulling her close, he dropped a kiss on her forehead. "I've missed you."

Slipping her arms around his neck, she pulled his head down. "That's no kiss…" she murmured against his lips."

"No?" he muttered, teasing her lips.

"Let me show you." She smiled before her soft lips met his.

They were just teasing, enjoying one another, but within minutes, he was burning up. His hands found their way underneath her top to the satiny softness he knew was hidden there.

With a sigh, she fell backward, pulling him with her.

Dinner was going to be late again.

CHAPTER 17

"See you tonight!" Jason called from downstairs.

"Okay!" Stacey had her hand in front of her mouth as she waited for the front door to close behind Jason. Even before she heard the thud, she was sprinting for the bathroom. She just made it to the toilet.

Minutes later, she sat weakly back on her heels. What on earth was the matter with her? She was never ill and she'd never ever been this sick before in her life. They'd had chicken for dinner last night...

Just the idea of food forced her to grab hold of the toilet again. This couldn't go on. She probably needed to see a doctor. As soon as she was back at work, she'd make an appointment. Apart from feeling like sleeping all the time, she'd also been strangely nauseous over the last few days.

Back in the bedroom, she put on her jeans and a top but it was a struggle. She was just so tired, even the simplest movement seemed to wear her out. She glanced at the bed. Maybe if she lay down for just a few minutes she'd feel better.

Quickly, she sent Billie a text, telling her she'd be late. There was so much work to do, but she wasn't going to get anything done feeling like this. It was Thursday, two weeks before Christmas, and the town was gearing up for all the festivities. They had to print flyers, make cards and a million other things, but just thinking about everything she had to do made her want to cry. She loved what she did. Why was she feeling like this?

Within minutes she was under the blankets again. If she lay still like this, she was fine. In just a few more minutes she should be ready to tackle the day. Her eyes closed and a light cloud picked her up. Sighing, she gave herself up to sleep.

A loud banging woke her up. She'd just fallen asleep a minute ago, who on earth…?

The banging continued and she sat up. At least she was feeling much better than before. As she got up, she looked at her watch. Oh, no! It was nearly twelve. She'd slept the morning away.

"Stacey!" Someone who sounded very much like Charlie was calling her name.

Why would Charlie be banging on the door? Combing her fingers through her hair, Stacey hurried out of the room and jogged down the stairs. When she opened the front door, Eleanor, Charlie, Lindsay, and Brooke were standing on her porch, all looking extremely worried.

"Are you okay?" Charlie asked immediately as she stepped forward. She placed her hand against Stacey's forehead. "No fever, that's a relief. Apparently, there is a nasty flu doing the rounds."

"I'm fine, but what are you doing here? How do you know—"

"We've been to your shop," Brooke interrupted her. "We were going to have hot chocolate at the coffee shop and was hoping you could join us."

"But then Billie said you sent a message to say you'll be a little bit late, but that was two hours ago," Charlie said. "She's also worried."

Frowning, Eleanor looked Stacey up and down.

"Sweetie, what's wrong? You look a bit pale."

"I… I'm not feeling so great," Stacey admitted. "But I'm sure it's nothing. I should probably make an appointment with the doctor, but—"

Charlie whipped out her phone. "I'll make the appointment, you go get your bag."

Jason wiped his forehead as he walked back toward his office after a class. He was out of breath, damn it. Probably because he hadn't been exercising as much as he used to before Stacey had moved in with him.

Going for a run was usually his way to unwind after spending a day teaching classes and tending to his ranch, but since Stacey was living with him, he'd been more interested in being with her than getting exercise. He grinned. It wasn't as if he was inactive, though. Making love to Stacey was a work-out, all right.

"Glad to see you're still grinning," Blake called out as Jason passed his friend's office.

Jason stopped at the door. "So are you," he teased.

Blake got up from behind his desk. "That's what the love of woman does to a man. So, what are your plans? The women have been wondering."

"Plans for what?" Jason asked.

"You and Stacey. Or is what you have a temporary thing?"

"Of course not. It's just…she and I need to talk, but there hasn't really been time…"

Blake shook his head. "Don't tell me you haven't even told her how you feel about her? Remember what I've told you about women and feelings? Talk to her, spell it out."

"She's not interested in marriage and babies, she's been very clear about that. I don't want to pressure her to do something she's not comfortable with."

"Talk. To. Her. Trust me, you'll thank me later. But before you do, you should probably make a trip to

Bozeman."

Jason frowned. "Whatever for?"

Grinning, Blake shook his head. "Oh, man. You do have a lot to learn. You wanna marry Stacey?

Sighing, Jason rubbed his face. "Of course, I do, but...what do I know about being a husband? Or a father? My dad walked out on us. Maybe I'm the same... She could do so much better than a cynical ex-FBI agent who—"

"That's bull and you know it," Blake interrupted him. "You were there when I nearly lost Lindsay because I didn't think I was good enough for her. Don't make the same mistake. Go for it. Don't hold back. Get a ring, get flowers, get whatever the hell you have to show her you love her. It's not difficult."

"Maybe tomorrow. I still have classes today..."

"Go. I'll take your classes."

"I don't know, man. Maybe I should talk to her first..."

"Trust me on this, okay?" Blake insisted. "We're not getting any younger. You don't have time to lose."

The idea had been to repeat to Stacey he never wanted to be without her again. He hadn't even thought of bringing up marriage, let alone babies. He still remembered what she'd said about her ovaries clutching her eggs every time she heard the word "baby," not an image he was easily going to forget.

Marriage? He'd always steered clear of entanglements, but since she'd moved in with him, he couldn't think of a life without her. He absolutely loved being entangled with Stacey.

Did he want to marry Stacey, though? Make babies with her? A million thoughts raced through his mind, all of them about her. For long moments, he tried to connect invisible dots. And then finally, he saw the picture so clearly: his heart had known this all long, he'd even told her—he never wanted to be without her again. So yeah, he wanted to marry her, make beautiful babies with her. Damn it, he loved her.

But he'd have to pull out all the stops to convince her. Nodding, he looked at Blake. "Okay, then. I guess I'm on my way to Bozeman."

Blake laughed. "The women will be so happy to hear this."

But Jason wasn't listening anymore. Hurrying toward his office, he started making plans. Should he let Stacey know he was going to Bozeman? Maybe not. Besides, the right words always seemed to evade him when he was talking to her. He'd much rather show her.

A ring and flowers shouldn't be a problem, but what else could he give her to convince her how much he cared for her?

As he grabbed the keys to his truck, his thoughts churned around and around until the idea was just there. Grinning, he jogged out to where his truck was parked.

He knew exactly what would make her happy.

As Stacey left the doctor's rooms, she was ice cold. She couldn't think. Her brain simply refused to work. One foot in front of the other, one foot in front of the other. Why couldn't she breathe?

Charlie, Brooke, Lindsay, and Eleanor immediately jumped up when they saw her.

"Stacey, sweetheart, you look as if you're ready to keel over," Eleanor said, rushing to Stacey's side. "Come and sit down. Whatever is the matter?"

Still dazed, Stacey shook her head. "Please take me home. My home." Her rental car was still on Jason's farm. She would have to get someone to go and fetch that. And her clothes. At this point more of her stuff was in Jason's house than in her own. She couldn't go back.

The four women were strangely quiet in the car. Charlie was driving and as soon as she stopped, Brooke jumped out and opened Stacey's door.

Feeling numb, Stacey walked toward the front door. Where was her key? It should be in her bag. Everything seemed to happen in slow motion as she searched for the blasted key. Finally, her fingers closed around it in her bag and she could unlock the front door. All four women followed her inside.

Charlie touched her arm. "Stacey, what is wrong? Please tell us how we can help you?"

Stacey sat down on the first chair, struggling to find the right words. Eventually there was just one way to say it. "I'm..." She had to gulp in more air. Oh, dear. Inhaling deeply, she tried again "I'm... pregnant."

A collective gasp sound went up in the air. Eleanor was the first to speak. "How...how do you feel about it?"

The sob Stacey had been holding in since she'd been with doctor, slipped out. "Petrified, but so, so happy!" she got out. "You know how I've felt about babies, but," she sniffled, "it has all changed, I've changed. Seeing Christopher, talking to the twins, making an appointment with the psychiatrist you've told me about, Eleanor, being with Jason... I don't know, somewhere over the last few weeks everything contributed to change my perception. I think... I... I'm ready to be a mom."

Charlie clapped her hands, Lindsay cried out and Brooke just hugged Stacey.

Eleanor's eyes were filled with tears. "Oh, sweetie, I'm so, so happy for you. So when are you going to tell Jason?"

Stacey shook her head, trying to keep the tears at bay. "I can't tell him! He doesn't want to get married, he's told me that on a number of occasions. I know he wants to be with me now, but that would change once his dopamine and norepinephrine levels settle, eventually. If he knows I'm pregnant, he'll feel it's his duty to ask me to marry me and I can never do that to him. I have to leave Alisson as soon as possible."

Charlie threw her hands in the air. "Are you listening to

yourself? Surely you've told Jason how you feel about him and he must've told you about his feelings for you. Anyone can see the two of you are crazy about each other. Talk to the man, please? Don't go jumping to assumptions."

Sniffing, Stacey dabbed her eyes. "He keeps saying we should talk, but I know he simply wants to make sure I understand the whole thing between us is temporary. And I don't want to hear that, so no, we haven't talked. I... I haven't told him I love him. Feelings are the last thing Jason will want to talk about."

"Oh, sweetie, I nearly lost Blake because we didn't talk to each other—" Lindsay began.

"So did Logan and I," Charlie said.

"And Gavin and I, too, nearly missed our chance at love," Brooke added. "We've all wasted so much time. Tell him how you feel, use the exact words."

Eleanor fidgeted with her bag. "I was so afraid Guy or I could die at any moment, I didn't want to acknowledge how I feel about him." She smiled tremulously. "But then he put on that monkey suit, as he calls it, to get my attention. Life is so very short, Stacey. Listen to your heart." She got up. "Come on, girls, I think we need to give Stacey time to breathe. You call us if you need anything, okay?"

One by one they gave Stacey a hug before they left.

Stacey grabbed a cushion from the coach and held it tightly against her body. She was pregnant with Jason's baby. A little human who would be totally dependent on her.

She waited for the panic to grab hold of her, but there was nothing. Just pure joy. She was going to be a mom. She was having Jason's baby. The overwhelming fear that she wouldn't know what to do, that she'd somehow hurt baby, was gone. But oh, her heart wanted to break.

Knowing Jason might not want the baby, should she listen to what her friends had said and tell him anyway? Or should she just pack up and leave? America was big. There were many other small towns she could disappear to.

With the cushion still hugged against her, she lay down on the couch. She was so tired; she was just going to close her eyes for a minute. Maybe her subconscious would come up with a plan.

He'd be such a great dad...

CHAPTER 18

By the time Jason turned into the ranch it was already dark. Everything had taken much longer in Bozeman than he'd anticipated. And the damn traffic and the many, many people were insane. Compared to much bigger cities, it probably wasn't that bad, but living in Alisson, he wasn't used to having to wait at a traffic light, stand in a line for anything he wanted—how did people live like that?

His phone had bleeped a few times and he'd noticed Eleanor had tried to call him, but if the message or call hadn't been from Stacey, he'd ignored it. Once things between him and Stacey had been settled, there would be enough time to talk, and apologize, to everyone else.

As he neared the homestead, he frowned. The place was dark. Not even the porch light was on. Where was Stacey? Panic gripped him around the throat. Had something happened to her? Where was she?

He probably should've sent her a message, but he wanted to keep the surprise until he was with her. He wasn't that late, but maybe she'd been worried...

As he stopped, another vehicle stopped behind him. Blake's truck. His breath hitched in his throat. This could only be bad news. Stacey... She'd been pale recently ...

Jumping out of the car, he hurried over to the other truck. But Blake wasn't in the car. Instead, Eleanor, Lindsay, Brooke, and Charlie got out. The expressions on their faces ranged from sympathetic to irritated.

"What the hell is going on?" he barked. "Where's Stacey?"

"If you answer your phone or look at your messages now and again, you would've known there was a crisis." Eleanor said.

"What crisis? Where is Stacey? Has she been hurt?" he cried out, really worried now.

Lindsay stepped forward. "Stacey is fine. Whether she stays fine depends entirely on you. Blake said you went to Bozeman today. Why?"

Relieved to know Stacey was okay, he exhaled. "Not that it has anything to do with the three of you, but I bought a ring and flowers and…well, a surprise, one that will hopefully be here before Christmas."

"You bought a ring?" Eleanor asked. "For…?"

Swallowing a cuss word, he glared at Eleanor. "Again, none of your business, but yeah, of course the ring is for Stacey. Damn it, she's living with me."

"Why did you buy a ring?" Charlie asked.

Baffled, Jason stared at the four women. There was a sub-conversation going on here, but he had no idea what it was. "Look, I know how she feels about marriage and babies, but I want her to know I'm ready to marry her if that's what she wants."

"So let me get this straight," Lindsay said, arms folded, "you've bought a ring for Stacey so that she'll know you're ready to marry you." She looked at the other three women. "He's missed a step, I think."

"Yeah, you've missed the most important step," Eleanor said. "Come on girls, let's go. This one he'll have to figure out himself."

They all moved to get back into Blake's truck.

Stunned, her stared at them. "Wait a minute. You

haven't told me where Stacey is. And what damn step are you talking about?"

Lindsay was the only one who turned around. "She's at her house. And the step you've missed? Tell her *why* you want to marry her. Hopefully when we see you at the Christmas Stroll tomorrow night, Stacey will be wearing your ring. Don't mess this up."

Before he could ask another question, Lindsay had gotten into the truck and they were driving away.

Damn it to hell. Why was Stacey at her house and not here? Hadn't he told her he'd always wanted her here, with him? What freaking step were these women going on about, anyway?

Muttering, he got back into his truck. He should've spoken to Stacey two weeks ago before she'd even moved in. But damn it, talking was the last thing on his mind when he was actually with her.

There was obviously some or other misunderstanding he was unaware of. As soon as he got to her house, they were going to talk about whatever it was that had made her leave the ranch, even if it took all night.

The baby was crying. Stacey wanted to go to her, but her feet felt like lead, she couldn't move. Nearly panicking, she kicked...and woke up.

For a moment she was disoriented. Why was she here, in her own house, and not on Jason's ranch? Her hand touched her belly even before she remembered.

She was pregnant with Jason's baby. She'd just heard a baby cry. Had she dreamed it? Smiling, she put both hands on her belly. It was a girl, she just knew it. She was expecting a little girl—one with her daddy's blue eyes.

Jason had to know about baby. She couldn't leave town without telling him. Marriage was not on the table, that she knew, but maybe he'd want to know about a baby, his baby? He should have the choice.

A loud knock on her door brought her out of her reverie. For a moment, she considered not answering, but the knocking continued. It was probably Eleanor with soup, or more motherly advice, or both. She could seriously do with any of those two at the moment.

Jumping up, she hurried to the door, combing her fingers through her hair. She had to be a sad sight. At least she wasn't feeling sick anymore.

She opened the door and froze. A haggard-looking Jason was standing on her doorstep with a ridiculously huge bunch of red roses and a big box, clearly with chocolates inside. Her heart kicked against her ribs, urging her to rush into his arms. She so needed his hug, but wordlessly, she opened the door wider. First, she had to tell him about baby.

"We have to talk," he said as he stepped past her into the house.

"I know what you want to say," she said.

"Oh, you do?"

"Yes, you want to make sure I know this," she motioned between the two of them, "is only temporary."

His nostrils flared. "That is not what I want to say."

She closed the door and walked back to the couch. Relief made her legs rubbery. She was struggling to breathe; it would be best if she sat down.

But...he wasn't going to tell her this, whatever they had, was temporary. A strange calm settled over her.

Jason put the roses and the chocolate beside her on the couch before he began pacing. "These," he pointed toward the roses and the box, "are for you. What is between us isn't damn well temporary. There is nothing fleeting about the way I feel about you. Those freaking levels you keep talking about? Well, mine is never going to settle down. We should've talked when you moved in but talking... I can't think when I'm around you, much less talk. Tonight, when I stopped in front of the house and it was dark and you weren't there...just the thought that for whatever reason you'd left, really freaked me out. I've told you I don't ever want to be without you again. So I bought roses, chocolates, and a ring today. Apparently red roses will send the right message. And okay, yes, I probably should've talked to you before I went to Bozeman, I don't even know whether you'll like the damn ring. I chose this one because it reminded me of your eyes." He walked toward her and sat down on the coffee table in front of her. "You have gorgeous eyes. Have I told you that?"

With her heart in her throat, she shook her head. The butterflies on her tummy were going berserk, her mouth was so dry, she couldn't possibly speak, and she felt so lightheaded, she was worried she was going to pass out and miss what he was going to say next.

He grabbed her hands. "I'm not good with words, Stace, so this may come out all wrong. I've never planned to fall in love, to marry, to have babies, but all of that changed when I met you. From the moment I saw you in my class, my heart was yours. I only realized it, though, when I was driving along Paradise Valley Loop the other day. I love you. I'm in love with you.

"I somehow never got 'round to telling you that in so many words, but I love you. I meant it when I said I don't ever want to be without you again. And yes, I know you don't want marriage and I do remember about your ovaries not wanting to let go of your eggs, and if you don't ever want kids, that's fine. But I want you to wear my ring anyway and whenever you're ready, you tell me and we'll get married right away."

He paused, his lips still moving a bit, and Stacey wasn't sure if he was finished with his speech.

Stacey exhaled slowly.

"Please talk to me? Tell me what I have to do so that you'll come back home with me?"

He'd talked so much. She'd never before heard him string so many sentences together but the only two words that had really registered were "ring" and "love." Had he actually said that, or was she still dreaming?

"Stace, babe, say something?"

"You love me?" she finally got out.

With his eyes never leaving her face, the beginnings of a smile finally curved the corners of his mouth upward. "I love you. You have my heart, always will."

"And you've bought a ring?"

"Yes." Cussing softly, he patted his pockets before he took out a small jeweler's box.

Her heart did a few cartwheels before it settled back. He flipped open the lid.

From a bed of black velvet, a beautiful square-cut blue stone, surrounded by tiny diamonds all around and down the side of the ring, winked at her.

With his heart racing, Jason watched all the emotions flitting over Stacey's face. Finally, he saw the one he was looking for: joy. But before he could take the ring out of the box and put it on her finger, she jumped up and began pacing. He waited.

Chewing her lip, she cast worried looks every so often in his direction. For long minutes he waited, his heart beating so loudly he was sure the whole street could hear it.

"Before I can say yes to the ring, I have something to tell you," she finally said. "You may change your mind when you hear what it is."

"I'm listening."

"I was going to leave Alisson without telling you, because you were very adamant about never getting married or having babies. I haven't wanted that either, or rather I never thought I did, but then you kissed me, you made love to me and I... I've fallen in love with you. And it's not as if I've planned it, I don't mean the falling in love part, although I haven't planned that either, it just happened, but I'm talking about the baby. Okay, you

ADORING STACEY

probably remember how adamant I've been about not
having babies, so you know I wouldn't have planned it.
We've used contraceptives since I've moved in with you
but that very first time…and there was the time in the
kitchen and then in the stables… Anyway, I'm pregnant.
I'll understand if you don't want to give me my ring, of
course I do, but—"

He'd jumped up when she'd said "I've fallen in love
with you," and by the time the word "pregnant" exploded
in the room he was right in front of her with the little box
still in his hand.

"You love me?"

She nodded, her eyes filled with apprehension.

"And you're pregnant?"

Her eyes narrowed. "If you're going to ask me if the
baby is yours, I'm going to slug you."

Swallowing his grin, he cupped her face. "I'm not
asking that."

"Good."

"So will you marry me?"

"You sure about that? It's not just me anymore."

"Stace, babe, I'm lost without you. I can't think of
anything more perfect than marrying you and raising
babies with you."

"I must warn you, though, raising kids is not easy.
Babies poop and the spit-up, and they need constant
attention. Toddlers make messes as far as they go, and—"

Nodding, he smiled. "I'm a quick study."

"And it's probably going to be years before you'll have
a proper night's sleep again."

"I'm sure we'll find something to do while we're
awake."

"You mean that?"

He didn't answer her. Instead, he took out the ring and
picked up her hand. "We've talked enough for one night.
Stacey Lawrence. Will you marry me?"

Blue eyes filled with a light he could only now

155

recognize. She really loved him.

But instead of throwing her arms around him as he'd hoped, she pulled back her hand, put it on her hip and cocked her head. "I don't know. I've never really thought about being proposed to, but shouldn't you be on one knee?"

"Are you serious?" he growled.

But she didn't budge. "I'm never doing this again. It has to be done right, don't you think?"

"You know I'm not a kid anymore?"

She chuckled.

With his eyes on her, he got down on one knee. "Stacey, will you please marry me? I think this is the third time I've asked you."

"Yes, Jason Coleman, I'll marry...oh!"

On the last word, he grabbed her hands and yanked her toward him. As she fell into his arms, he moved and gently put her down on the carpet.

"I haven't thought this would be so hard," he grumbled as he took out the ring. His fingers were a bit unsteady as he slid the ring into place. It was a perfect fit. "Sapphires," he said as he brought her hand to his mouth, "it had to sapphires like the color of your eyes." He pressed his lips against her finger. "And now I want to make love to my future wife." He slipped a hand under her top. The next moment his hand froze. "What about baby?"

"We won't hurt baby," she whispered as she pulled his head down.

Deep in the night, Jason turned so that he was lying behind her. A big hand slipped around her waist and he touched her belly. "You're pregnant."

"I'm pregnant."

He chuckled. "So those ovaries finally let go?"

Still half asleep, she hugged his arm. "I'm not even freaked out. I... I think it's a little girl. I dreamt about her

156

just before you knocked on my door."

"A little girl?" he said. "She'd have your red hair and we'll get her a dog. I also had a dream."

"Really?"

"It was such a clear picture."

"It's too soon to really tell, I think, but... I was thinking, shall we call her Margaret? Your mom's name?"

He didn't answer, just buried his face in her hair.

"We can call her Maggie," she said, "but I don't know if we can tell people we've named her after your dead truck."

Laughing, Jason flipped her on her back and hoisted himself above her. "Life with you will never be boring." With a sigh, he slipped into her.

Tucked close under Jason's arm, they joined their friends on the Christmas Stroll the following night as they all walked down Main Street toward City Hall. A deep sigh slipped out and Stacey dropped her head against Jason's strong body. She still wanted to pinch herself. She couldn't believe how blissfully happy she was.

Jason hugged her close. "Last year this time, you wouldn't even look at me," he teased.

"I was trying to stay out of your way, remember?"

"Oh, yes, you were trying to settle those chemical levels you went on about."

Grinning, she buried her face in his coat. "I was so sure the crazy feeling I got whenever you were around was only biology. If I wait for my dopamine and norepinephrine levels to settle, I'll be over you."

"So how are those levels doing?" he teased.

She laughed. "I'm pregnant. My hormones are all over the place as you very well know."

"I love my insatiable fiancée," he whispered in her ear.

Her heart tripped. She was never going to get enough of this man.

"Eleanor, no!" Guy's voice reached them and Stacey and Jason stopped.

Charlie and Logan with little Ellie, Lindsay and Blake with baby Laney strapped around him, and Brooke, Gavin and Connor turned around.

"Mom?" Brooke asked, looking from Guy to Eleanor. "What...?"

"We're getting married on Christmas Eve," Guy said. "I'm not waiting another day."

"But...it's three days from now, why the hurry?" Eleanor tried.

To their astonishment, Guy bent down and kissed Eleanor soundly. "Because, Eleanor, I've been waiting for you all my life. I'm not waiting another day. Charlie and Logan agreed to have it on the ranch."

"Why is grandma kissing Mr. Richard, Mom?" Connor whispered loudly.

Guy patted Connor on the head. "Because I love her, son. Eleanor?"

"But I..." Eleanor began heatedly.

"But you what, Eleanor?" Guy was clearly at the end of his tether. "You either want to marry me or you don't."

"I do!" Eleanor cried out, "But I... I don't want to leave my grandkids!"

Guy's smile was triumphant. "Well, then, we won't have a problem. Logan and I talked. I'm buying shares in the ranch and if you don't mind, I'll be moving in with you."

For once, Eleanor was speechless. "You'll do that?" she finally got out.

"I love you, woman," he said and pulled Eleanor close again. "Why is that so hard for you to understand?"

"Well!" Brooke said as the rest of them left the older two people behind. "Never thought I'd see the day our mother is speechless. So, Guy talked to you?" she asked her brother.

Logan grimaced. "I don't know who was more

embarrassed, him or me, but hopefully we'll never have to have that particular conversation again."

"Oh, you men." Charlie sighed. "Why is it so difficult to talk about your feelings?"

"It took Jason a while, but when he finally shared his feelings, he didn't want to stop," Stacey teased.

"I was told," Jason said, pointing at Blake, "women like to talk about feelings."

"We do, indeed," Brooke chuckled. "Talking about feelings—I'm in some serious need for hot chocolate. We have another wedding to plan. And ladies, tomorrow morning, we're driving to Bozeman for Mom's dress. I'm going to need all the support. You simply have to cancel any other plans you have and come with us. She's not going to want to buy something special."

As they made plans, Stacey peeked at Jason, but he was talking to Blake. She was wearing his ring, she'd agreed to marry him, but since they'd gotten engaged, he hadn't mentioned getting married again. Hugging his arm, she smiled. She couldn't really be bothered about papers, anyway. She knew her man loved her, and that was all she really cared about.

ELSA WINCKLER

CHAPTER 19

Brooke was right. From the moment they drove away from Alisson the following morning, Eleanor had tried her best to persuade Brooke she didn't want another dress. She tried manipulation, and when that didn't work, she pleaded. When she realized nobody was listening to her, she'd grumbled.

It was nearly lunch. They were all tired, hungry, and thirsty but by the look on Eleanor's face, it was going to take a miracle to get her to buy a dress.

"Come on, Mom," Brooke said as she took Eleanor's arm. "Just this one more place, okay? I'm sure we're going to get the perfect dress for you here. And then we can go and celebrate with a lunch."

"I have many dresses I can choose from…" Eleanor tried again. "Really, Brooke, I'm over sixty. Nobody cares what old people wear."

"And since when are you old? Maybe other sixty-year-old women age, but never you," Charlie said. "The men are on baby duty; we have all day to find you something. Come on, when last have we girls been able to get away together and shop?"

Stacey swallowed a laugh. Eleanor had no chance with

Brooke, Lindsay, and Charlie on a mission to find her a wedding dress.

"I don't know why Guy is in such a hurry to get married," Eleanor muttered. "Why not wait until the new year? There is just three days left 'til Christmas Eve."

"You've organized weddings in less time," Brooke insisted as they entered the beautiful shop filled with wedding dresses.

Looking stricken, Eleanor made a U-turn. "I'm not wearing a white wedding dress!" she said adamantly.

A friendly looking lady approached them. "Good day, ladies, my name is Grace. How can I help you today?"

"My mother is getting married," Brooke said, a hand firmly on Eleanor's arm.

"I'm sorry we've bothered you," Eleanor said. "You obviously won't have anything for someone my age."

"On the contrary!" Grace smiled. She winked at Brooke, Lindsay, Charlie, and Stacey. "Why don't you ladies make yourselves comfortable and you," she said, gently taking Eleanor's arm, "come with me. I think I have the perfect dress for you. You are such a beautiful woman…"

As she led a worried-looking Eleanor away, Brooke sagged down on one of the chairs. "Thank heavens they have chairs," she groaned, rubbing her back. "I've forgotten how tired being six months pregnant makes me. How are you feeling, Stacey?"

Stacey smiled as she also sat down. "Very happy to be able to sit down. Fortunately, the worst of the nausea seems to be gone but I just want to sleep."

Charlie and Lindsay were looking through the wedding dresses. "Oooh, Stacey, you should have a look at these dresses. You're also getting married soon, aren't you?"

While Charlie was talking, Stacey's gaze fell on a blush-colored tulle dress. "I like that one," she said as she got up and walked toward it. "It's a skirt, though, not a dress," she said as she took it off the rails.

Just then Grace appeared. "Eleanor is trying on a very special number. I think she's going to look lovely. Oh, you will look gorgeous in that with your red hair." She smiled at Stacey. "I have the perfect top to go with that," she said as she took a top in a softer shade of blush from one of the racks.

"It's a cross-over, Stacey," Lindsay said. "It's a sign. This is your dress…"

"What do you think?" Eleanor asked from behind them and they all turned around. She looked stunning in deep, dark red velvet dress.

For a moment there was a stunned silence.

Eleanor turned around quickly. "This is silly, I'm…"

Brooke was the first one to speak again. "Mom—you look…" She sniffled as she got up and rushed toward her mother. "You look amazing. Absolutely amazing, and I'm buying you this dress."

"Of course, you won't…" Eleanor tried, but Brooke shook her head.

"I really want to do this, Mom. Please let me?"

"We have shoes to match," Grace said, as she produced a pair of velvet slippers in the same deep red as the dress.

"Logan and I will get that for you, Eleanor." Charlie said immediately.

A clearly overwhelmed Eleanor burst into tears.

"Oh, no, Mom." Brooke sniffled as she hugged her mother. "I'm pregnant, I cry about everything. Don't get me started!"

As Stacey looked for a tissue in her bag, Charlie handed her one. Everyone had tears in their eyes.

"Here we go," said Grace as she entered carrying a tray with a bottle of bubbly and a bottle of juice. "The juice is for the pregnant ladies."

"I understand how you know I'm pregnant," Brooke laughed, "But how did you I'm not the only one?"

Grace pointed toward Stacey. "She's glowing. Of

course she's pregnant."

"Before you can have juice, just put on the skirt and top," Charlie said.

"I don't know…" Stacey muttered, lifting the skirt up again. "It's beautiful but it's probably way too expensive. And besides, I don't even know when we're getting married."

"Just try it on," Lindsay said. "It such a great idea for a wedding dress, I'd love to see it on you."

"Okay, I'll try it on, but I'm not buying anything today. We'll probably only get married sometime in the new year."

Minutes later she stared wide-eyed at her reflection in the mirror. Growing up, she'd never even thought about weddings and dresses and rings, and now look at her. Not only did she have the most gorgeous ring on her finger, but she was also trying on wedding dresses.

The skirt and top fitted perfectly. As thoughts of Jason raced through her mind, she twirled in front of the mirror.

I want you to wear you my ring anyway and whenever you're ready, you tell me and we'll get married right away. Out of breath, she stopped and laughed. Those had been his exact words. He'd given her a ring. He'd told her it was up to her to decide when.

Grinning, she opened the curtain so that she could show her friends the dress. It was going to be a challenge to get everything ready in time, but fortunately, she was extremely good at organizing.

It was close to six o'clock on Christmas Eve when Jason stopped in front of Logan and Charlie's homestead on their ranch. Stacey had left early that morning. She'd been helping Brooke, Lindsay, and Charlie to prepare for tonight's wedding.

It had been a long day without her. He was used to having her around. The ranch was just not the same when she wasn't there. Over the last few days, she'd decorated the house for Christmas—not something he'd ever done. Doing Christmas with Stacey, though, was fun. She'd insisted on a Christmas tree and last night they'd started to decorate it. They hadn't gotten very far before they'd ended up naked in front of the fire.

Rubbing his chest, he couldn't help smiling. To his utter delight, they always ended up naked.

As he got out of his truck, he glanced around at all the vehicles already parked in front of the house before he checked his phone. He'd hoped Stacey's surprise would already be here. No message, though. Hopefully everything would fall into place soon.

Waving to the few people standing in front of the house, he jogged up the stairs to the porch.

Everyone living in or near Alisson was here. Both Eleanor and Guy were beloved and respected members of this town, and the news of their upcoming wedding had spread like wildfire. Since yesterday morning, the ranch had been a beehive of activity. Everyone had pitched in to help make this day memorable for the two people who'd found one another late in life.

As he stepped into the house, he blinked. The place had been turned into a Christmas Wonderland. He'd thought Stacey had gone a bit overboard decorating their house for Christmas, but this was next-level.

Fairy lights hung from the ceiling, a big Christmas tree took up most of the one corner in the living room, and every possible surface had some kind of Christmas ornament on it.

Charlie was coming down the stairs. "Jason!" She was a bit out of breath but smiling. "Just the person I was looking for. Stacey is asking for you. Upstairs, first door to your right."

Taking the steps two at a time, he hurried toward his fiancée. He couldn't wait to see her again.

"Stace?" he asked as he opened the door, and promptly

lost his breath.

In a floaty pinkish skirt made from layers and layers of some or other soft material, and a cross-over top that hugged her breasts in all the right places, she was devastatingly beautiful. "Wow..." With two steps, he was in front of her. "You look stunning," he murmured as his hands slid down her arms.

"Uhm..." she began, and for the first time he noticed the slight tremor on her bottom lip.

For some reason, she was nervous. Frowning, he cupped her face. "What is wrong? Is baby...?"

"Baby is fine, I'm fine. I have to tell you something."

"Of course."

Biting her lip, Stacey inhaled a few times before she looked him in the eye. "I...it sounded like a good idea at the time, and everyone else thinks it can work, but now I'm not so sure. But you did say I should tell you and well, I'm telling you now."

"Stace, babe—what are you talking about?"

"Do you remember what you said when you gave me my ring?"

"That I love you?"

"About getting married."

"I said..." And then the penny dropped. His heart thudded so loudly, he struggled to hear his own words. *I want you to wear my ring and to tell me when you're ready to get married.* "But babe, haven't you already agreed to marry me?"

"Yes, but...you haven't said *when* and I... I don't want to wait another second. I want to get married to you today."

It took a few seconds for his befuddled brain to understand what she'd just said. "You and I are getting married today?"

Her eyes bright, she nodded. "After Eleanor and Guy have tied the knot, of course. I was worried I'd steal their moment, but they're leaving around eight, right after the ceremony. They're catching an early flight tomorrow morning and will be staying in Bozeman tonight. So I thought…everyone is here, why not get married? That is…if you still want to?"

Grinning, he kissed her softly. "Well," he drawled. "I don't know…"

Frowning, she tried to pull her hands out of his.

"You see, I've been told," he said touching her face, "a marriage proposal has to be done while on one—"

Even before he'd said "knee," she was down on both knees. "Damn it, we don't have much time. Will you please marry me tonight?"

Laughing, he grabbed her hands and pulled her up. "I was thinking we'd do it on New Year's Eve, but tonight sounds perfect." Cupping her chin, he took in everything about the face he'd come to love so much—her gorgeous blue eyes, the satiny texture of her skin, the spattering of tiny freckles over the bridge of her nose, her long, red hair falling in curls down her back, her soft mouth. "I love you, Stace. Always will."

"And I love you," she smiled, her eyes brimming with tears.

Worried, he wiped away the lone tear running down her cheek. "Why the tears?"

"Happy tears," she whispered against his lips.

Relieved, he pulled her closer and kissed her.

A loud knocking on the door interrupted them. "Someone downstairs is looking for Stacey," Lindsay called out.

"I have to put on lipstick again." She smiled as she pulled herself out of his arms.

"I'll wait for you downstairs," he said. "I also have a surprise for you. Not to boast or anything, but I do think my timing is perfect."

"What are you talking about?" she asked as she turned toward the mirror.

"It's a surprise!" He winked as he opened the door.

Before he walked out, he looked over his shoulder. "Stacey?"

Smiling, she looked at him in the mirror. "Yeah?"

"You've made me a very happy man. I can't wait to show you exactly how happy."

Blushing, she smiled.

As Jason left the room, Stacey had to clutch the chair to stay upright. What the man could do to her knees with just one smoldering look...

With a last glance in the mirror, she left the room. She was in her wedding dress, getting married to the love of her life that night. Swallowing against the lump in her throat, she started down the stairs. She would've given anything to have her mom and dad here tonight, but hopefully, they were looking down on her and they were smiling.

Before the last step, she looked up and nearly lost her balance. A grinning Jason was standing next to her cousin. "Christopher! What on earth...?"

A beautiful young girl moved forward. "Hi cuz!" She smiled.

"Penny?" Stacey gasped and she rushed forward. "Is that really you?"

"What about me?" the handsome young man on Jason's other side called out.

"Kevin?" Stacey whispered. Overwhelmed with joy, she looked at Jason. "But how...?

"Told you I also have a surprise for you." Jason smiled.

With a cry, she hugged her cousins one by one. "This is so perfect, I—"

"Ladies and gentlemen," the local pastor called out. "Please take your seats, we're about to begin.

Jason took her hand and with her three cousins following them, they found seats. Maybe she should pinch herself just to make sure this was really happening.

"You okay?" Jason whispered as they sat down.

"I'm excited, I'm happy, and just want to cry," she whispered back. "Happy tears," she said quickly when he frowned.

"I still have to get used to those." He exhaled. "I can't wait to take you back home," he whispered as Guy joined the pastor in the front.

As the first notes of music filled the room, everyone got up and turned around to catch a glimpse of the bride. A regal-looking Eleanor entered, her hand tucked into her son's arm, her gaze on the man waiting for her in the front.

"I'm so glad I've found you before I've turned sixty," Jason whispered and he put an arm around her.

"We're the lucky ones," Stacey muttered as they all watched Guy walking forward to meet his bride.

Logan shook Guy's hand and kissed his mother before he joined Charlie and Ellie in the front row. Guy picked up Eleanor's hands and just looked at her.

The pastor cleared his throat, but Guy wasn't to be rushed.

"You look beautiful," he said before he pulled his bride closer and kissed her soundly. Everyone laughed and clapped hands.

It took a long while for everyone to settle down so the ceremony could begin.

ELSA WINCKLER

CHAPTER 20

"You may kiss the bride!" the pastor finally called out.

Jason squeezed Stacey's hand. "It's nearly our turn," he said softly. "You ready?"

Her eyes sparkling, she nodded. "So ready."

Meanwhile, Guy had pulled his bride close again and amid shouts and whistles, was kissing her. A blushing Eleanor finally stepped away and with Guy's hand in hers, she took the microphone from the pastor.

"There is going to be another wedding just now," she announced. She turned to look at Jason and Stacey. "Jason and Stacey, I know you wanted to do this after Guy and I have left, but I can't miss out on seeing the two of you get married."

She waited for the excitement to die down before she continued. "I've been called an interfering old busybody, but when I see two people who so obviously belong together like Stacey and Jason do, I feel obligated to make sure they end up in the same room together. I've had to think far outside the box with these two." she smiled. "Stacey was a hard nut to crack. But then I had the idea of the bachelor auction..."

Inhaling sharply, Stacey looked at Jason, who was

grinning. "She told me it was someone else's idea," she whispered.

"It's time to 'fess up," Logan called out. "You've played matchmaker before, haven't you?"

Eleanor smiled at her son. "Are you and Charlie happy, Logan?"

"Blissfully so!" they called in unison

"What about you, Lindsay and Blake?" Eleanor asked.

Lindsay and Blake laughed. "Yes!" they shouted.

"And my darling daughter Brooke and Gavin?" Eleanor smiled.

Gavin and Brooke lifted their laced fingers in the air. "Thank you, Mom," Brooke said with a laugh.

"Well, then, my work is done."

"So why did you give me such a hard time?" Guy asked out loud.

Eleanor gave him a cheeky smile. "I married you, didn't I?"

Amid the laughter, the pastor tapped on the microphone. "So do I understand it correctly, we're doing the second wedding right now?"

"Please," Eleanor said. "Stacey, Jason—come on, you two."

With Stacey's hand in his, they walked to the front. As they took their places, he looked down at their laced fingers. He didn't know why he was so lucky to get to marry this woman, but for the rest of his life he was going to make sure she knew how much he adored her.

Hours later, Stacey joined her cousins at their table. "My poor feet!" She sighed.

"You and Jason make such a cute couple." Penny smiled. "Oh, Stacey, I'm so happy we're here. Kevin and I have talked about you so much over the years. You were such an awesome babysitter. And now you're having your own baby—how do you feel about that?"

Stacey laughed. "A bit freaked out, I must admit. But knowing that Jason will help me makes all the difference." She touched Penny's shoulder. "I'm so happy you guys are here. Please tell me you're not leaving too soon?"

"Jason has invited us to stay on the ranch, but that was before we knew you're getting married," Kevin said. "Won't you be going away on your honeymoon?"

"Only in the new year," Jason said behind her as he put his hands on her shoulder. "So you are welcome to spend as much time with us as you want."

"That would be so great," Christopher said, looking over Stacey's shoulder. "But now I'm going to dance. I see the cute waitress I've met in the bar the previous time I was here. So excuse me!"

"He's a fast worker." Penny chuckled.

"If you know, you know." Jason said, taking his bride's hand in his. "I have one more surprise for you."

Smiling, Stacey pressed a hand to her abdomen. "I don't know if the butterflies on my tummy can handle any more surprises."

Jason pulled her close. "I adore you, Stacey, and tonight I want you to know exactly who I'm singing to," he said, as he took the microphone the lead singer of the band handed to him.

He pulled her closer and with his eyes on her, he opened his mouth.

I'll never not love you

Around them, people started clapping, but Stacey didn't pay any attention. Because she'd been ignoring her heart for such a long time, she'd so very nearly let this man slip through her fingers.

Moving into his arms, she put her head on his chest.

The tough time she'd had growing up had brought her here, to Alisson. The last thing she'd expected when she'd arrived in this quant town was that she would fall in love and heaven forbid, have a baby.

Jason's love had made all the difference.

As the last notes of the ballad died down, he bent down and amid more cheering, kissed her.

Eleanor sniffled. "See? What did I tell you? They belong together. Okay, husband, I'm ready. We can go now."

"About time. Come on, wife." Guy took Eleanor's hand in his. As they headed for the front door, everyone grabbed a coat and followed them outside.

A full moon shimmered against a cloudless sky and the blanket of stars spanning the sky winked and glittered, creating a glorious Christmas Eve show.

As Guy and Eleanor drove away, Stacey's family and hers and Jason's friends gathered around them. Stacey couldn't stop the tears.

"Please tell me those are happy tears?" a worried Jason asked as he tried to wipe them away.

"Very happy tears." Stacey sniffled as she stepped into his arms.

When she'd moved to this little town all those months ago, she hadn't known she was embarking on a whole new life.

One filled with friends, family, laughter—and the love of good man.

ACKNOWLEDGEMENTS

I would like to thank Melissa Keir and Inkspell Publishing for making this series possible. It has been such fun to work with you.

Also a big thank you to each and every reader who buys and enjoys the stories. I so appreciate your lovely messages and positive feedback.

And as always thanks to my own live hero who keeps supporting me and who still reads every word after all this time – you are one of a kind.

DON'T MISS THE OTHER BOOKS IN THE UNEXPECTED LOVE SERIES

KISSING CHARLIE: #1

One Kiss Will Change Their Lives Forever

Bowen therapist Charlie Wilson is not interested in men or relationships. Her only concern is making sure her sister Lindsay is safe.

But then billionaire Logan Johnson walks into her rooms and stirs powerful feelings inside of her. Logan's perfectly knotted tie is a clear indication free-spirit Charlie should steer clear of him at all costs.

They are complete opposites, so why does he keep coming back to see her?

EXCERPT:

"How did you hurt your back?" Her voice was cool, and she wasn't meeting his eyes.

"While hiking," he said curtly. He was in pain; it didn't matter what the hell happened. "Tell me about this

Wowen, Bowen, whatever the hell you call this cr—therapy."

She gave him a cool look. "It's called Bowen Therapy."

"Bowen Therapy," he said, his gaze on her mouth.

"The guiding principles of the technique were established by Tom Bowen during the 1950s. It focuses on the whole person, not just the condition. In other words, it treats the cause, not only the symptoms. It helps the body to heal and restores the balance by shifting the body from your innate 'fight or flight' system to a more natural state of calm."

He watched her as she studied his body. She was holding something in her hand. Damn, she had yet to touch him, but he was struggling not to react to her nearness. The fact that he was lying on his back wasn't helping, either.

"Natural state of calm? With you doing strange things to my body?" he grumbled, only realizing the ambiguity of his words when they hung in the air around them.

Her lips twitched.

"Oh, you think this is funny?" he snarled.

"I think you're in pain. I think you like being in control and at the moment, you're not. That's why you feel the need to lash out. But it's fine. I often have children throwing tantrums."

"I'm not throwing a tantrum, damn it…" He tried to sit up straight, but a pain shot up his back, and groaning, he had to slowly lie down again.

"The movements in Bowen Therapy," she continued as if he hadn't interrupted her, "are very distinctive and are used on precise points on the body. It involves moving the soft tissue in a particular way. I will use a rolling-type movement, using my fingers, hands, or sometimes my elbow. It will create a focus for the brain by stimulating the nerve pathways and tissue. I work on only a small area, depending how far your skin can move. What you may find strange—"

"This whole damn day is strange. I don't know what the hell my mother was thinking," he muttered.

PROTECTING LINDSAY: #2

How does he protect his heart while protecting her?

Lindsay Wilson simply wants to concentrate on her shop where she sells her own mixtures of creams and essential oils. What she doesn't want is the seriously sexy Blake Davidson hell-bent on protecting her from the abusive boyfriend who followed her to Montana all the way from South Africa. To add to her frustration, he makes her feel things she's never felt before but she's made a mistake in the past, can she trust her instincts this time?

Blake lost two people before because he couldn't protect them, so what's different this time with Lindsay? From the moment he's laid eyes on her, all his instincts have been telling him to make sure nothing happens to her so he has no choice but to move into her place and keep her safe. But what about his own heart?

EXCERPT:

For the first time, she really looked at him. Oh, my. He'd grown a beard since she'd last seen him. She'd never liked beards, but on this tall, dark, and ridiculously attractive guy, it only added to his smoldering good looks.

Grinding her teeth to make sure her jaw wouldn't drop, she turned away. "So, which essential oils are you interested in buying today?"

Here she was, a grown woman, just about salivating because a gorgeous man was in her shop. Maybe she should seriously begin to think about dating again. "There is an essential oil for just about every problem you may have. Suzie's husband, for instance…" The minute the words left her mouth, Lindsay nearly groaned out loud. Normally, she kept clients' issues completely confidential, but Suzie had already let that cat way out of the bag. Even so, why talk about Suzie's bedroom problem, of all things, while she was talking to Blake?

"I don't have problems in the bedroom." His voice was as smooth as Tennessee whiskey.

Lindsay closed her eyes for a minute. He didn't have to tell her that; one look at his broad shoulders, square jaw, and confident stride made it clear he was all man and… Oh, my goodness, the very last thing she should be thinking about was Blake and bedrooms.

"Okay, so maybe something for your beard?" Why didn't she simply shut up? She motioned to one of the shelves. "I make a very nice oil with lavender, peppermint, lemon, and coconut oil. You should try it."

"I don't…" he began gruffly, before he swore softly and took out his wallet. "Okay, give me the damn oil."

LOVING BROOKE: #3

Can two friends fake love or will their fake relationship end their real friendship?

Irritated by their families continued efforts to get them together, good friends widow Brooke Johnson and Gavin Wilson decide to fake a relationship for the next two weeks. But then Gavin kisses her, making her aware of the desires she'd suppressed for so long.

Suddenly, Brooke struggles to focus on finishing paintings for an upcoming exhibition and her simple life becomes way more complicated than before.

When a creepy gallery manager makes her life unpleasant, Gavin wants to take control of the situation and red lights flicker. Brooke had made a vow to handle her own problems rather than relying on someone. Her husband's death had left her in the dark about finances. She couldn't let Gavin take over but will their new romance stand up to her hands off attitude? Or will Brooke learn that it's okay to lean on the ones you love sometimes?

But in the small town of Alisson, Montana, love will find a way.

This classic friends to lovers and fake relationship story will be sure to delight fans of Nora Roberts and Susan Mallery. Come be swept away, today, by this amazing story!

EXCERPT:

"What...what are you doing?"

"I'm going to kiss you. Two reasons: one, I've been thinking about it all night, and two, then we'll know." By the time he'd finished speaking, his lips were trailing down her face.

She caught her breath. "Know what?" she whispered, unsure of what she was asking.

"Whether we can pretend to be more than friends."

His lips had reached her ear. Desperately, she tried to stay focused, but her eyes closed, sending her other senses into overdrive. The subtle scent of sandalwood seeped through every pore of her body, the sound of his uneven breathing left goosebumps all over her skin, and the feel of his stubble against her cheek had her blood roaring in her ears.

And then his lips touched hers—just briefly before he lifted his head again. Those impossible blue eyes were looking right into her soul.

"What do you think?" he asked.

"What do you mean?" Was the husky voice hers?

"I mean," he said, pulling her closer, "do you think we'll succeed in pretending to be a couple?"

Before her muddled brain could make sense of his words, his warm, wet mouth was on hers again. Oh, my goodness, the man knew how to kiss.

Available Where Books Are Sold...

ABOUT THE AUTHOR

Elsa has been reading love stories for as long as she can remember and when she 'met' the classic authors like Jane Austen, Elizabeth Gaskell, Henry James, The Brontë sisters, etc. during her English Honours studies, she was hooked for life.

She married her college boyfriend and soul mate and after 46 years, 3 interesting and wonderful children and 4 beautiful grandchildren, they are now fortunate to live in the picturesque little seaside village of Betty's Bay, South Africa.

She likes the heroines in her stories to be beautiful, feisty, independent and headstrong. And the heroes must be strong but possess a generous amount of sensitivity. They are of course, also gorgeous! Her stories typically incorporate the family background of the characters to better understand where they come from and who they are when we meet them in the story.

Webpage: www.elsawinckler.com
Personal Facebook page:
https://www.facebook.com/elsa.winckler
Author Facebook page:
https://www.facebook.com/ElsaWincklerRomanceAuthor?ref_type=bookmark
Twitter: https://twitter.com/elsawinckler @elsawinckler
Goodreads:
https://www.goodreads.com/author/show/6557709.Elsa_Winckler
Pinterest: http://www.pinterest.com/elsawinckler/
Wattpad: http://www.wattpad.com/user/elsaw1
Instagram: https://www.instagram.com/elsaw1/